Blanket

A Boy and His Dog (A Series of Short Stories)

Dr. Richard "Rick" Rhodes

authorHOUSE®

AuthorHouse™
1663 Liberty Drive
Bloomington, IN 47403
www.authorhouse.com
Phone: 1 (800) 839-8640

Published by AuthorHouse 01/29/2016

ISBN: 978-1-5049-7602-2 (sc)
ISBN: 978-1-5049-7603-9 (e)

Library of Congress Control Number: 2016901517

Print information available on the last page.

PROLOUGE

I

This book is especially dedicated to my special longtime friend, Neal Ahern, the SPCA (Society for the Prevention of Cruelty to Animals). To PETA (People's Ethical Treatment to Animals). To Neal and Jenny's beloved dogs, whom my wife Gwen and I truly adore; Wegi, Peaches, and the late Checkers: To Thomas and Fran; their beautiful collie Tommy: To Jeanette; the late Max our neighbor's little dog: To Bontia's dogs; Charley and Wonder: To my nieces Pheetta and Susan's dogs; Pepper and Appollo: To Greg and Becky's new puppy; Sunny To Bev and Ralph's dogs, Bentley & Bailey: To Karl and Thelma's dogs; Guci, Coey and Shasha: To Mary and Sam Smiley's dog; Banjo: To my friend Don's dog; Cee Cee. To Jerri and her dogs; Autum and Rocky: To Jaun's dog; Miley: To Bob and Paquita's; cat Gracie: To pet lovers and Veterinarians all over the world, "THANKS."

Congratulations to Jane Smiley, Achieving
Her Veterinarian License

*Special thoughts to my son Dusty and Debbie's
dogs, Nikko, Rokko, China and cat, Coco.*

*My daughter Rikki and son-in-law Greg
and their dog, Mikin and cat Nox*

*Remembrance to my beloved late dogs:
Duchess, Skipper, Mike, Jacco, Kiki, Max,
Dancer and Maverick*

*This book was inspired by a very close lifelong friend
of mine, Neal Ahern and his dog "Wegi," who would
visit me and my wife Gwen at our lakeside home each
weekend, we were close by neighbors. Wegi always expected
an early morning treat and was the first to arrive,
Neal trailing behind for his treat, a beer or two.*

*A small English "Harrier" Fox Hound.
Easy to track a faint scent for hours and maintain it.*

Courtesy
"THE DOG BREED"

Dr. Caroline Colie, Ph.D Published By "BARRON"

SPECIAL ACKNOWLEDGEMENTS

II

GWEN RHODES   *Technical Advisor, Consultant,*
                                   Encouragement

RIKKI RHODES   *Assistance*

SIMONE WILSON   *Playwright*

MICHAEL "HAP" O'DANIEL *Mentor/Writer/Journalist*

ALEXANDER O'NEAL   *Author/Writer/Guidance*

SPECIAL THANKS

Three Beautiful Lovely Ladies, MAESOA DARTON, KATHERINE CLARKE & JOAN WARREN for Advice and Inspiration.

REVUES

INTRODUCTION

IV

"BLANKET"

A BOY AND HIS DOG

BLANKET – Jona's dog wants to be pleasing. He loves to be petted, praised and rewarded. He has not been to obedience school but follows commands due to Jona's training. From his running barking, jumping and playfulness you can tell he is a happy dog. Faithful to Jona, though seldom when scolded he has that pitiful head down, lay down look, meaning, "I'm Sorry." Within minutes, even seconds he's pawing on Jona's leg wanting to jump into his lap for forgiveness. Again he displays he is Jona's "Best Friend.

JONA – Twelve years old, long brown unmanageable hair, evenly cut over his forehead can't recall his name or why he is in this situation. Jona's personality is typical of most twelve-year-old boys, not many worries. He likes to laugh, ride his bike and most of all play with his dog. Gets into very little trouble. His "Best Friend" is his dog. He's very close to his parents whom are very loving and understanding. He has many friends, likes school and gets average grades. He's not very athletic but likes sports. His dog was a birthday present from his parents, there could have been no greater gift. He and his dog have a "loving" Relationship.

THREE LEGS – Small Brown Bear injured from hunter's trap on one leg. Becoming what they first believe him to be an aggressive enemy. After their short distant encounter, they begin to trust one another. Together they form a close loveable relationship, a TRIO, they begin to communicate through barks, growls and human language, claps, hand signals and petting.

They begin to survive as a team, a threesome after each one's tragic ordeals. Eventually Three Leg's wound is healing though he limps off into the wild everyday but returns. Some time with fish or berries. Blanket begins to chase rabbits for food unsuccessfully in the beginning, no matches Jona has to practice building a fire from scratch.

TABLE OF CONTENTS

PART ONE

PART TWO

Jenny and Neal and Wegi

PART ONE

"THE ORDEAL"

A weekend camping trip was just what they all needed. A little time in the northwest wilderness to bond and enjoy Jona's childhood before he grew into a teenager and had little interest in time with his family. His father Alston and mother Denise, Aunt Carol, Uncle Les and his dog. Driving their loaded SUV through the woods; Jona, his parents, aunt and uncle, and the boy's dog arrive at a choice spot to set up a campsite. Here, the thick trees thinned. The dense underbrush became sparse and left nothing but high grass and a few wildflowers in and almost perfect circle. Perhaps the rangers had cleared the area for camping. Or maybe it was a small pod long since dried up and overgrown with what little vegetation carpeted the area. Either way, it was the perfect spot. The SUV they had driven in wouldn't make it much further seeing how the trees on the other side of the clearing thickened and there wasn't much by way of a path other than the subtle trail from what little foot traffic came through the area.

It was perfect. The SUV was loaded up with all the necessities, but they had still brought tents and knapsacks. It wasn't "roughing it" without at least forsaking the car for more outdoorsy quarters. Jona helped his dad setting up the tents while his mom and aunt unloaded some of the cooking utensils and his uncle searched for firewood. It wasn't long before camp was set and with the sun threatening to set in a few hours, all were eager to explore the area before bedding down for the night.

They set off hiking. Jona and his dog lagged behind: playing, throwing and retrieving sticks, and a little bit of roughhousing. The others; his parents, aunt, and uncle came to a large rocky overlook. It seemed a fitting place to stop and rest while they waited for Jona and his dog to catch up to them. They smiled and chatted as they pointed to distant sights on the horizon.

The sun, moving closer to the peaks on the other side of the valley; the serpentine river wound its way through the middle of the scene. "Fit for a postcard!" his aunt chimed as she began snapping photos with the new camera she had bragged about all the way up the mountain. "Oooo! Over there, Dear" his mother cooed pointing toward some other area of interest as she leaned into his father, linking her arm to his.

Suddenly, the ground began to tremble. Jona watched in fascination as tiny pebbles bounced and jittered across the path. His dog sounded a low moaning howl, turned his head upwards before a more violent tremor came to an abrupt halt. The dog seeming shocked at the earth slipping beneath his feet. Next, he was barking furiously towards Jona's family, Jona turned, running toward them just in time to see his parents, aunt, and uncle disappear. He fell striking his head on a large rock rendering him unconscious for a short period; coming too, the dog licking his face and pawing at his body. Some of the earlier events are somewhat vague to him, the campsite, where he is, his dog's name; bewilderment, shock and devastation overwhelm him. Suddenly the ideal weather instantly begins to change. Heavy snow and wind, temperatures' dropping below zero. He is not adequately dressed for this weather. He can't recall the direction of the campsite. The snow has become almost impossible to walk in.

Disoriented, freezing and about to give up, they find little relief under a low cave like rock shell. Gathering his thoughts, his mission is to find the campsite and survive.

Leaving the shelter, treading the deep snow, lost and wandering, they survived the cold miserable night. The morning sun brings some comfort.

Vaguely, Jona recalls a campsite again, confused, lost and wandering, his mission is to find it and survive. Treading through the deep snow, mostly in circles, they come upon a small brown bear. His leg is caught in a hunter's steel trap, which is chained to a nearby tree. Jona and his dog relate to the bear's pain from the trap and his struggle to release itself. They become helpless observers.

After many frustrating attempts to free the aggressive injured bear, at some point it seems they begin to develop a sort of human-animal relationship, as if the bear understands they are trying to help him, a rapport or communication begins to set in. Jona at a certain point finally gets close enough to release the bear's leg from the trap. Immediately, Jona and his dog flee from the bear. Without Jona's knowledge, the bear follows them from a distance, undetected. After a short distance, they become aware of the bear's presence, which seems to be at this point the bear is more passive than aggressive.

Jona becomes more cognizant of the bear's behavior. However, in his frustration and fear, gives up his state of mind, he goes berserk, picks up a stick, turns to challenge the bear, screaming, come on, claw us, kill us, eat us." The bear stops in its tracks, lowers its head in a passive, cowardly stance. Jona now realizes the bear is no longer an enemy or aggressive threat to him or his dog. Maybe even a friend! Jona, tired, cold, frightened and again frustrated turns his back to the bear walking away, head down, crying, stating to himself, "You Three Legged Bully."

Eventually that becomes the bear's name, "Three Legs." Finally, they form a threesome. They begin to communicate by barks, growls and human language. They begin to survive as a team.

Three Legs walks around ahead of them, leading them to a small cave for some but little comfort, much better than the elements they were previously exposed to. Three Legs wound is slowly healing although he still walks with a slight limp. The three of them snuggle close at night, Three Legs in the middle providing body heat for warmth to Jona and his dog.

Three Legs disappears each day, returns with a fish taken from a nearby stream. No way to start a fire, Jona can't recall his brief scouting experience days, raw fish becomes the daily menu. The dog trying to compete with Three Legs, jumps into the stream to catch a fish, almost drowns, comes out shivering, his short haired coat covered with slivers of ice but he survives. So he begins to chase rabbits to catch for his contribution to the trio, unsuccessful at first but finally he becomes a novice at the challenge. Jona however begins to experience early signs of malnutrition. Though the nearby stream is abundant with fish, only Three Legs can catch maybe one a day. After many attempts Jona gets a fire started by rubbing sticks, no knife, they cook fish, but eat the rabbits, fur burned and all, better than nothing. Three Legs disappears from time to time and returns with a small limb bearing wild berries.

The dog also begins to disappear from time to time, the first time he returns with an icy snow covered blanket. Jona vaguely begins to recall bits and pieces of his past, recognizes the blanket. He remembers the disappearance of his parents, which brings deep emotional suffering and unstoppable tears. In his mind, he visualizes the soft warm bed in his room. He realizes the dog has found the campsite, however coaxing the dog to lead him to it is of no avail.

Time after time, the dog disappears, returning with a Blanket, sometimes another item such as a skull cap that Jona remembers is his, Jona rewards his dog with pats, praises and hugs each time. The dog happily jumps up and down on Jona's leg knowing he has done something good.

The disturbing point is each time the dog brings something from the campsite, dragging the blanket covers up his tracks, the new fallen snow covers his tracks.

Remembering his beloved parents, he takes on the task and goal, which is the most important journey of his life, survival. This returns his strength and courage for whatever lies ahead. He vows to himself he will get out of this demoralizing, dangerous and life threating situation. He has prayed constantly, both day and night for someone to save them. Will his prayers ever be answered?

Days and nights have passed. It is still snowing profusely, too deep for him to tread through. The dog takes off to return with another blanket, same results his tracks are again covered with snow. Where has he been Jona wonders?

Disgusted, freezing and in pain, he builds a snowman to have an imaginary person to talk to. Another day, the dog romps off again, returns with another blanket from the campsite. This particular day the snow has somewhat dissipated, enough so that the dog's tracks can be followed. Jona and Three Legs take off following the dog treading ahead, through the melting snow. The dog leads them to the campsite. Extremely overwhelmed and happy, Jona begins to celebrate, rolling in the snow, yelling happily, the dog and Three Legs seem to understand this is a special day, barking and growling they also begin to roll in the snow.

They now have food, flashlight, matches, cooking utensils, etc. The event however is short lived.

Jona begins to have temporary flashbacks of his past experience, his parents' disappearing before his eyes, the entire camping party, and the beautiful overlook has turned ugly in his mind. Grief, sadness and despair set in.

As Jona's mind begins to somewhat clear, he finds some solace in the fact that he has not only saved his life but his dog and Three Legs, in fact, they have all saved each other. The "SUV" is unlocked but no key to start it, Jona doesn't know how to drive anyway. They pitch a tent and snuggle, as they are use to by now. This time the fire outside keeps them warm and more comfortable, noting they haven't been comfortable at all before.

The snow, even though somewhat melted over the days has made the tire tracks invisible. Therefore, Jona doesn't know which direction they should travel for help. The only clue is the rising and setting sun. Jona is plagued with many questions but no answers. Now more than ever his mind is filled with confusion. Should they leave the vehicle and choose the wrong direction, only to find the three have wandered further into the wilderness? How long would the food last? No more raw fish and burned furry rabbits. They now have food. What if there is another snowstorm! It would cover their tracks from a search party. Finding the campsite to this point has been extremely lucky. Not to have been succumbed to the elements of the wild or dangerous animals, maybe because of the presence of Three Legs.

The funny thing is as Jona opened the tailgate of the "SUV" Three Legs is trying several times to climb in with his injured leg and large clumsy body, however he finally makes it, (determination).

Suddenly there's the sound of helicopters overhead, then the sighting. Joy and happiness, jumping, barking, growling and happiness again as if Three Legs understands, maybe he does! Jona, with tears coming from his eyes realizes this is "bittersweet." He's losing more than just a friend but a dear great friend. Reluctantly he shoos Three Legs off before the rescuers arrive, good-bye Three Legs, GOD bless and we love you.

After a successful rescue, an evaluation and medical exam Jona and his dog are placed in a temporary shelter home. His dog often retrieves blankets from other rooms, expecting to be petted and rewarded as before.

Not having total recall of past events, his dog's name, etc. Jona names his dog "BLANKET."

Jona in solitude thinks to himself, where was GOD? Was HE that enormous storm, snow blizzard or the sunlight that cleared the skies so rescuers could find them and save three lives? If all these things, good or bad were you GOD, he thinks to himself "THANKS FOR BEING THERE."

"PLACEMENT"

Jona and Blanket, after being rescued are placed in a temporary replacement center until Family Services and other authorities develop a plan for a permanent placement.

The couple, Mr. and Mrs. Burgin, in their late fifties, a White middle class Christians, retired, no children, have temporarily taken Blanket and Jona into their home and been very caring to both of them.

They develop a soothing rapport in a short period of time, they become some-what of a caring family. Jona is somewhat content but not really happy. How can he be? He recalls to often the loss of his parents and his tragic ordeal. He often has memories of Three Legs and wonders what he is doing, has his leg healed?

The Burgins are pleased about the new experience of becoming parents. They realize it is temporary. Prematurely they begin to think of adoption. Quickly disappointment sets in. Family Services informs the Burgins that through intensive investigation, they have found a biological relative of Jona's, he is Jona's father's cousin, very wealthy. Jona has never heard of him. Family Services decides it would be in Jona's best interest to live with this newfound relative.

The Burgins are deeply saddened by this news. They feel in a way they have been betrayed. They begin to dwell on their loss. Slowly anger sets in. They feel they should have been compensated for taking Blanket and Jona in. After all, they had become very fond of Blanket and Jona, why weren't they given consideration in this decision, to them it was like stealing Blanket and Jona. Slowly they become more angered, frustration sets in. Their minds begin to develop a plot in retaliation. Kidnap Jona, hold him for ransom, after all, this new found relative is rich. After all, the ransom money in turn would in some way satisfy their disappointment and loss.

Pheetta and Pepper

"THE PLAN"

First, find out where Blanket and Jona are living! Next, Surveillance! Three, gather as much information as possible before execution of a plan.

The Burgins', realizing they are not criminals and cannot perform the actual abduction and kidnapping, they need to procure an undesirable element they believe they can trust. They think of this plan as a scheme rather than a criminal act. They have always considered themselves to be good Samaritans, not criminals. After all that's what they were when they took Blanket and Jona into their home.

Now the search begins for accomplices. Mr. Burgin is visiting and getting acquainted in area bars he has never visited before. Eventually he befriends a frequent customer he believes would be receptive to his plan and could be trusted. After continuous visits he confronts a patron of the bar; a male, White, mid- thirties, scrubby appearance, his name is Ruddy. At the Burgin home, they further discuss the plan with now two accomplices, Ernie, also, male White, fortyish, potbelly always wearing dirty coveralls a friend of Ruddy has enlisted in the plan. The Burgin's inform them of the ransom plot and the money involved and each one's share.

Jona and Blanket are transferred to an interim location until arrangements are in place for them to stay with his newly found relative. Geographically, Jona and Blanket have relocated to a warm climate, this is satisfying to them. They never want to see snow again. Meanwhile, the Burgin's have had no problem finding their location. Ruddy and Ernie are studying Jona and Blankets routine habits.

Jona and Blanket have discovered a special somewhat secluded area with a shallow stream in a small wooded area where they wade and splash water on each other. The place is picture perfect and soothing to them. After days of surveillance, the accomplices feel this is the perfect spot for the kidnapping. Eventually the opportune time arrives.

After playing in the water, Jona is sitting on a log, Blanket by his side, oblivious to the fact someone is in their presence. Jona is attacked from behind and physically restrained. Duct tape placed over his mouth, Blanket is barking loudly and snapping at one of the kidnapper's pant leg, he also is grabbed, restrained, and hand muffled. Both are dragged off struggling and thrown into a red van with door lock restraints. Jona is crying, screaming, "What are you doing?" Blanket is again barking loudly knows something is wrong. Before the final destination, the van pulls to the side of the road, Blanket is thrown from the van. Jona has been blind folded, however before Blanket is thrown out he is on his hind legs, looking out, again pawing and scratching at the windows as he has done in certain situations before, sensing something is wrong. A phenomenon, not understood by humans, but by animal instinct, Blanket after a couple of days finds his way to his temporary home. The ransom call however, was initiated several hours after the kidnapping. The police were notified, a search party has been organized and the FBI has become involved.

Moving the unsuccessful search from the town to surrounding suburbs, Jona's relative's hope of the enforcement authorities finding Jona is rapidly dwindling. He has anxiously been awaiting Jona and Blanket's arrival; he realizes Jona is his biological relation, real family. Blanket has been placed in the back of one of the deputy's search cars. Again, Blanket is on his hind legs looking out the window, paws against the window hoping to see Jona, whining and pawing. The deputy's pull into a Mini-Mart service station requesting the attendant to put a poster up with Jona's picture on it, the attendant complies. Exiting the station, a red van is gassing up.

Blanket jumps from the search car, runs to the side of a van, begins barking and pawing on its side. He starts running around the van, barking, circling it displaying erratic behavior as he has done in other unusual situations.

The deputy's and his partner, not having knowledge of Blanket's behavior are upset at the dog. As they enter their vehicle, Blanket does not respond to their retrieval commands. Finally, they get out of the car and retrieve Blanket. They think to themselves, something is wrong with this dog, strange, they think, stupid! Due to their law enforcement instinct, they decide to run the license plate. The owner's name is Ruddy Austin, ironically, his address is in the same town where Jona and Blanket lived with the Burgins. The driver of the van emerges from the rest room, finishes gassing the van. They follow the van to a house somewhat secluded at the edge of town. At this point, they don't know what to think or expect. After a short period of time another car arrives, they run a license check on the plate. Shockingly to their surprise, it is registered to the Burgins.

They call for back up, other officers including the FBI respond, they organize and close in on the home. Announcing themselves, they enter, find the Burgins, Ruddy Austin and another individual named Ernie Wells causally sitting around the living room, excitedly surprised, jumping up as the officers enter. Blanket immediately runs barking towards a room at the rear of the house, again scratching and pawing on a locked door. Breaking in, they find Jona hands and feet tied; all the windows are boarded up preventing any attempts of escape. Blanket and Jona are happily reunited, barking, hugging, Jona is crying aloud, Blanket, Blanket, Blanket. All four individuals are arrested. They are charged with a felony Conspiracy of Abduction and Kidnapping.

Jona's testimony in court was a horrific ordeal for him. After all, he had grown very fond of the Burgins. Returning home, again Blanket greets Jona, Jumping, barking and running in circles. Happiness, to a Boy and his Dog.

Dusty and Nikko

"FAMILY UNITED"

The newly found cousin Blanket and Jona have been placed with is a male White, forty-year-old, Mr. Jason Reynolds, handsome, average height, frequent smile, dimples below each cheek easy to like, Jona bares a slight resemblance to Jason. After a short period of time, Jona begins to affectionately refer to him as "CUZ". He is receptive and pleased with the nickname. He lives in the small lakeside wealthy community of Lake Shore, it has narrow asphalt roads, grassy on the sides, very little traffic and great neighbors. Decorated with a variety of assorted trees, a large lake, boat docks beautiful landscaped homes. An abundance of wildlife. This is paradise to Jona and Blanket.

Blanket and Jona take a routine walk every morning getting familiar with the neighborhood. They become friendly with an elderly retired couple, the Randolphs', they have no children or pets of their own, they become very attached to Blanket and Jona. They have a treat awaiting Blanket every morning. Jona doesn't walk Blanket, Blanket walks Jona. As they near the Randolph's house Blanket always takes off running, leaving Jona behind, expecting his doggie treat. Jona, not far behind receives his treat also, usually a breakfast roll or cookies and milk.

On this particular morning, very close to arriving at the Randolph's house they pass two men walking on the other side of the road. Lakeshore is a walker/jogger's heaven. Blanket begins to follow them, barking angrily and aggressively, (animal instinct)! Finally, he obeys Jona's command to come back.

Jona is upset at Blanket's behavior, he scolds Blanket, he has never been aggressive towards walkers or joggers before.

Just as they are approaching the Randolph's house, as usual Blanket takes off running for his morning snack. The screen and front doors are closed, Blanket runs to the back deck to sliding glass doors, no response, he begins barking and pawing on the glass, puzzled!

As Jona arrives, he experiences the same results. The Randolphs only have one car, it's in the driveway. Jona circles the house, the boat is at the dock. Jona thinks to himself, someone must have picked them up and taken them someplace. They continue their walk.

The next morning, same routine walk, no response at the Randolphs, now Jona thinks, maybe they left town, but why wouldn't they have mentioned it? Jona inquires of the next-door neighbors, the Whitney's if they have seen the Randolphs. "No". They respond. They inform him, if the Randolphs were leaving town they would have told them. Next morning, same results, Jona becomes curious, circling the house, scratching his head and returning home he informs Cuz what has been happening. At first Cuz dismisses Jona's report. He then realizes Jona is very concerned, he calls the police to console Jona. The police arrive and interview Jona, they respond to the Randolph's house, knocks on front and rear doors, no response. They question neighbors, the next-door neighbors inform them if the Randolphs were leaving town they would have informed them as usual to keep an eye on the property. They have seen no movement; however, the houses are some distance apart. The police, now suspicious, proceed to enter the residence forcibly.

"GOD", two dead bodies in the bedroom, murdered, bludgeoned. The house has been ransacked. Finding no next of kin, the neighbors, reluctantly identify the bodies. Nothing seems to have been taken, maybe money or jewelry, however a small floor safe is ajar, no signs of forced entry, the police go through the safe, find nothing of value.

The police retrieve Jona and Blanket; bring them to the house for questioning believing they may be some help to them. They keep Jona from crossing the crime scene tape not wanting him exposed to the horrific scene inside; however, Blanket takes off running through an opened door expecting a treat, sniffing around, puzzled again. He is immediately shooed off by the homicide detectives who have arrived at the scene. Unknown at this time, Blanket has picked up a scent. At this time, there are no suspects. The investigation continues.

The small community, learning of the tragedy becomes concerned about their own safety and welfare. Nothing has happened like this before. Not even misdemeanor crimes.

The police are frustrated, dead ends. They decide to interview Jona again to see if he recalls anything strange or unusual that first morning. Results are negative. As the police are leaving, Jona, for some reason has flashes of Three Legs. "Oh wait" he calls out "What?" The police respond. "That first morning, those two walkers, one of them walked with a limp, it came to me when you said the word unusual, unusual behavior for Blanket." I remember, the one with a limp had on a blue ball cap, I think a grey shirt, the other a plaid –like lumber shirt, blue jeans, I think, I'm not sure, one had on white sneakers, I don't know, I think the other had on sort of work pants with the straps over the shoulders, I don't know.

They go back to the house, maybe Jona can recall more. On the short walk to the house at a certain point Blanket runs across the road, sniffing, barking and running in small circles, he doesn't retrieve to Jona's call back, this time they cross the road to get Blanket, he's sniffing around a small area with tire tracks, the spot is damp but not muddy, also there is a cigarette butt on the ground. Jona informs them, this is the spot Blanket was barking at them.

The detectives think something here! Forensic is called to the scene, they take a plaster cast of the tire tracks, photographs and take the cigarette butt for DNA testing in case of future suspects. The main question is, "Why this particular house?" The detectives praise Blanket realizing Jona has an exceptional dog. Everything is taken to the forensic lab to be analyzed. Later, the forensic report informs them Mr. Randolph apparently put up a weak struggle, minute pieces of skin was found under one of his fingernails. This is extremely good news towards future investigation. All of the evidence is taken to the property room to be preserved for the continuous investigation.

Cuz informs Jona he's taking him and Blanket to a small nearby town, Keyser to visit an old friend for the weekend. It's a very short drive with beautiful scenery. Cuz believes this would be a fun weekend for Jona, easing some of his sadness, depression and memories after everything he has been through. Cuz and his old college roommate Grady decide to invite some of the neighborhood kids over and have a cook out and swim party for Jona and Blanket. They make a grocery list and add the necessary items needed. After shopping the friend suggest they take a stroll up and down the main street of the small town. Walking back to their car, Blanket takes off running, barking at an individual exiting a tavern, snapping at him. Jona states, "There he goes again." The individual angrily and loudly states to Jona, "Get a lease for your mutt." Jona embarrassingly apologizes. Picking Blanket up walking back to Cuz and his friend, Jona looks back, watching the individual cross the street, Jona notices his slight limp. "My GOD", he thinks to himself, "That's the limp."

Jona runs back to Cuz and Grady informing them of his thoughts or even suspicions. They observe the individual enter a white pick-up truck, on the door is advertised, "Halls Home Maintenance" and a phone number. (002) 431-0906. A query of the license plate reveals the owner's identity.

Cuz knows Jona by now, his wit and integrity, he informs Grady they need to leave immediately; cutting their visit short, returning home and personally informs the police of their experience. One of the detectives recalls retrieving from the safe a manila envelope, a contract proposal with the name "Hall's Home Maintenance", a phone number, however, Mr. Randolph's signature was not on it. They contact the authorities in Keyser, meet them and go to Mr. Hall's home to question him. Mr. Hall, early thirties, slightly overweight, brawny looking is very calm, he informs them he has several employees that use the company truck from time to time. He doesn't know why it would be in the vicinity of Mr. Randolph's home or whatever his name is. He doesn't know why he would have one of his contract proposals.

The police procure a list of his employees, take pictures of all four tires on Mr. Hall's truck, permanently mark them. Forensic gets a perfect match from one of the tires. "BINGO."

Mr. Hall has a slight limp. After interrogating each of the employees, one is extremely excitable and nervous. Ronald Adams, he has some traffic violations, that's all. After a fingerprint comparison, the prints from the crime scene match his.

After a lengthy interrogation, confronted with the evidence, he confesses, also his DNA matches saliva on the cigarette butt. Found on the roadside, also the brand name is identical.

Adam's story: Mr. Hall and he went to the Randolph home to get him to sign the contract to do the home remodeling work. Mr. Randolph informed Mr. Hall he was getting another contractor to do the work. Mr. Hall said he was counting on the money, physically pushing and pushing Mr. Randolph from room to room.

We had seen the safe previously while inspecting what was to be done. Mr. Hall forced Mr. Randolph to open the safe, Mr. Randolph began to struggle, his wife physically tried to intervene.

Mr. Hall took his hammer from his tool belt and began striking Mr. Randolph and his wife who tried to stop him. I don't know why we parked the truck where we did, just up the road. Mr. Hall went through the safe taking money and jewelry. He gave me two hundred dollars and told me I didn't see anything.

The authorities arrest Mr. Hall. The DNA test results from the skin under Mr. Randolph's fingernails matched his. Jona could not identify either man. Mr. Hall was arrested, charged with Aggravated Homicide, eventually convicted, Adams was charged and convicted as his accomplice.

Another great job by Blanket. Jona felt some gratification, but will still have fond, but bittersweet memories of the Randolph's, maybe Blanket will miss them as Jona does! Jona gave a small party for Blanket, tied a scarf around his neck which Blanket didn't like, Cuz gave him a new leash which he didn't want and never used, a nice collar he loved, an abundance of snacks.

Did Blanket know what all of this was for! We'll never know.

"A Boy and His Dog"

"SOAP POWDER VS. COCAINE"

On occasion Blanket still chases rabbits without success, it seems he has fun doing so. He still obeys every one of Jona's commands except in unique, suspicious circumstances.

Jona is becoming more aware of Blanket's behavior when something is wrong. He begins to realize Blanket is not an ordinary dog as the detective told him, Blanket is exceptional. He has a natural instinct to pick up a scent and track it.

After Jona experienced the tragic loss of two of his fondest friends, the Randolphs. He and Blanket chose a different walking routine as not to pass the Randolph's house. They began to walk the coves on another area of the lake. Eventually it becomes soothing, except no more snacks for him and Blanket. Sadly, Jona keeps remembering the Randolphs.

The different walks become routine. Jona and Blanket have fun, skipping stones across the water, splashing, throwing and retrieving broken tree limbs. Happiness begins to fulfill them. Past tragedies they have not forgotten but seems to somewhat fade from time to time.

On their new walking route, each time they pass a particular boat dock, Blanket seems to act uneasy, somewhat excited, nothing to pay any attention to.

On a particular morning walk, as they reach the dock Blanket is sniffing and barking. Jona commands him "Come Blanket, come on." Blanket hesitantly obeys Jona's command, they walk on. A couple of mornings pass, as they are approaching the dock a male White possibly in his twenties, dressed fashionably sportsman like, exits the house carrying a plastic grocery bag. Blanket runs ahead of Jona, as he approaches the male he begins barking, growling and snapping at the man. Jona gives Blanket a "No, No" command, Blanket doesn't obey. The man viscously swings the plastic bag at Blanket slapping him in the face. Blanket snaps at the bag tearing a small corner, a small amount of white powder streams out. Blanket runs back to Jona exerting a loud squealing bark.

After this short encounter, Blanket runs back to Jona. They both do an about face retracing their walk. Jona is thinking why such a fuss over a little bit of soap powder.

As Jona is looking back, he observes the man talking to himself angered and using profanity and scraping up the small amount of powder with his hands and fingers. Blanket and Jona turn their walk into a run. Shortly they forget the incident. Being apprehensive, they wait a couple of days before resuming their walks. Periodically Jona notices a different boat at the dock. Blanket still acts unusual each time they approach the dock. Occasionally Jona would observe the same individual coming out of the cove, each time in a different boat, angrily staring at him.

Finally, Jona mentions the encounter to Cuz who pays attention to Jona, he becomes somewhat concerned. Cuz ask Jona to tell him everything he remembers in detail as he recalls them. Cuz realizes a twelve-year-old could not make up a sequel of events such as these. It ponders on and irritates Cuz's mind. He thinks, have Jona and Blanket stay away from that particular cove or walk it half way, but this wouldn't be fair. Cuz feels somewhat uncomfortable. His mind circling in thought, why get so upset over some soap powder? Starring angrily at Jona after such an encounter would not seem unusual to carry a grudge, somewhat normal. Shortly Cuz's concerns fade away.

Cuz needs to go to the marina to buy a few fishing accessories. Jona and Blanket love to be on the boat fishing with Cuz. While waiting in the car Jona observes the individual from the encounter at the cove coming from the boat rental, as he approaches them Jona nervously slides down in the boat.

He peers over the dashboard and watches the individual put the same type plastic bag in the trunk, return to the boat rental and briefly return and drive off. He excitedly informs Cuz what has taken place, Cuz is helpless to do anything, but has some concern for Jona's state of mind.

A short period of time goes by. Cuz is grocery shopping, he runs into Mr. Detective, they greet. Mr. Detective asked, "Hi, how are Jona and my favorite dog doing?" Cuz replies, "Fine a few minor incidents here and there you know youngsters." "Yeah like what?" Mr. Detective inquires. Cuz informs him of what has been happening. Mr. Detective, scratching the back of his head as though he has curious thoughts in the back of his mind. He asks Cuz if he could stop by sometime and talk to Jona. "Sure, anytime." Cuz replies. Mr. Detective meets with Jona and interviews him about his last incident. The results of which seem to require further investigation. They have received anonymous calls from a couple of lakeside residents about different boats pulling up to the same dock for very short periods of time and leaving. Mr. Detective's instincts kick in (white powder, white powder) "Huh", he thinks to himself, drugs, drug trafficking, no! The thought irritates him like gum sticking to his shoe. Since Jona has observed this same individual exiting the boat rental, that's a place to start.

Mr. Detective and his partner Josh begin their investigation by locating the anonymous callers from across the cove, their information supports Jona's story. The next step is to interview Mr. Owens the owner of the boat rental, he is very cooperative. He informs them the same individual rents a boat two or more times a week. The normal minimal rental time is two hours, what's unusual is he has the boat back within fifteen minutes to a half hour, no fishing equipment. Mr. Detective and Josh review the boat rental records. It reveals no driver's license or credit card was ever used, the individual always paid with cash.

Mr. Detective and Josh consider three options:

One: Have Mr. Owens call when the individual rents his next boat, that won't work, they could not respond in time.

Two: Borrow a boat from the owner, anchor in the cove posing as fishermen (a stake out) take pictures of the individual leaving the house with a plastic grocery bag.

Three: Surveillance at the marina each day, look for an individual exiting a fishing boat with the small plastic grocery bag, procure the license number, follow the car to its destination, however because of Mr. Detective and Josh's time restraints and radio calls it would be difficult.

Four: Request Cuz, Jona and Blanket to stake out the parking lot at the marina, better yet, have Mr. Owens call Cuz whenever the individual rents a boat, they're less than ten minutes from the marina, and they could get the license number and follow the car to its destination. That works!

Several mornings later, Mr. Owens calls Cuz and informs him the individual has rented a boat. Cuz, Jona and Blanket drive to the parking lot waiting for the individual to return. He exits the boat he goes directly to his car in the parking lot, puts the bag in the trunk, and then returns to the boat rental. Cuz gets the number of the license plate, follows the car to its final destination, the address, 612 Parker Drive, Norway, South Carolina. The small town of Norway borders the Lake Shore community. They relay the information to Mr. Detective and

Josh. The license plate is registered to one Thomas Davies, male, White, 27 years of age, a one-time convicted drug dealer. They procure a photograph from NCIC and data of Davies past criminal history, mostly misdemeanor arrest.

At police headquarters, the detectives show Jona a picture, Blanket is sitting on Jona's lap.

Jona identifies the person Blanket had he encounter with as the same person exiting the boat and putting the bag in the trunk of the car. Blanket begins barking loudly. The detectives jokingly state, "Wonder if Blanket can identify someone without sniffing!"

A search warrant is procured for the lake house Davies has been frequenting; also the house at 612 Parker Drive. Requesting support from neighboring law enforcement agencies, they set up a synchronized raid on both houses, the precise time is arranged when they believe everyone will be home. This way one location cannot notify the other location.

After more investigation, it's time for a search warrant. Since the community has a minimal police department, officers from adjoining communities are called in for support. The raid is set-up. Cuz, Jona and Blanket are allowed to be distant observers. The raid is extremely successful, almost three million dollars of cocaine (street value) is recovered. Cuz, Jona and Blanket are let into the house to observe the finale of the operation.

In the basement of the Parks home, in a small cupboard they find a table with a glass top, used for cutting, small amounts of cocaine residue, a scale and other utensils used to cut drugs. The owners William and Doris Parks are arrested and charged with Drug Trafficking.

Leaving the house Blanket again won't respond to Jona's retrieval command, he is barking at a small radiator with grid holes in it just above the floor baseboard. Cuz, Jona and the detectives are familiar by now, when Blanket displays erratic behavior. Inquisitively they pry open the radiator, "shocked," they find a pound bag of cocaine wrapped in a plastic grocery bag.

There is a special community celebration, everyone attends. Jona and Cuz are presented with plaques for community service. Blanket is presented with a ribbon around his neck, hanging from it is a metal medallion. Blanket is standing on his hind legs turning and barking, He's Happy.

Does Blanket know what this is all about?

"A Boy and His Dog"

"HOME INVASION"

It's a weekend, Jona and Cuz are sitting on the sofa in the game room very much enjoying themselves playing video games and eating popcorn and snacks. Blanket is lying at the end of the sofa stealing a cornel of popcorn every now and then. The doorbell rings, Cuz states, "I'll get it." As soon as Cuz gets the door ajar, two young male Whites force their way in, one of them carrying a revolver uses it, knocking Cuz to the floor. Cuz screams for Jona to run, inquisitively Jona runs into the room, both he and Cuz are subdued, tied to chairs with their mouths taped.

Their legs are tied to the chair legs, hands tied behind them around the back of the chairs. The intruder with the gun is tall, white, stringy black unkept hair stringing over his forehead, the other, male white is somewhat stubby, bald, big chunk of tobacco protruding from is left jaw, stuttered speech; both have stubble beards, scroungy dress. The taller seems to be in charge.

The intruders demand to know where the safe is, Cuz replies, "There is no safe." This is not true, Cuz has a medium size safe in a closet in his bedroom. Blanket is running around snapping and barking at the intruders, the unarmed intruder is chasing Blanket trying to catch and muzzle him.

Blanket is too fast and small for him; he repeatedly chases Blanket from room to room to the third floor where Blanket has his own small cubbyhole with a small crawl space, where from time to time he seeks his solitude. He becomes quiet and stops barking. After several attempts the intruder is tired and worn out, he is frustrated and angry.

The intruders begin taking extremely expensive paintings from the walls not realizing their value. Eventually a further search reveals a small safe in Cuz's bedroom closet. The intruders request the combination, Cuz refuses and gets slapped hard several times. He is bleeding from the fore head from being knocked to the floor by the gun. They continually slap him in the face and punch his body.

Cuz has two expensive cars parked in the driveway, a Ferrari and a Mercedes, expensive boats at the dock. Jona is extremely frightened, scared to wits end with tears streaming down his cheeks; observing Cuz being punished, blood trickling from his nose, a bruise beneath his eye. Eventually, after Cuz's refusal to reveal the combination the intruder's assault escalates. The intruders are larger than Cuz but not by much. Cuz is a religious physical fanatic and martial artist. Cuz is helpless with injuries from the beatings, weak, and thirsty. He becomes desperate to scheme or plan in some way for him Jona and Blanket to escape this terrible ordeal.

Cuz now recalls at the last Lake Shore Community Meeting the residents were verbally informed there were several home robberies in the area, even a printed notice was put up. He thinks to himself, before the Randolph incident there was never any serious crime at Lake Shore; only a few petty incidents caused by juveniles. Now he realizes he should have been more concerned, he's angry with himself. His thought at the time like everyone else is, not going to happen to me.

Now he is concerned about his neighbor, Miss Fran coming over with a snack of some kind, which is not unusual, and becoming a hostage and his girlfriend Roberta whose plan is to come over and cook a special meal for Jona, himself and a snack for Blanket. Cuz is hoping this doesn't happen. They could be assaulted or even sexually molested by the intruders.

During this entire incident, Blanket periodically comes downstairs, barking and being chased.

The intruders unplanned plan is becoming more of a failure, unraveled, they begin arguing and snapping at each other, more and more frustrated, undecided what to do next. The unarmed intruder, tired of chasing Blanket tells his companion to shoot Blanket the next time he comes downstairs. The armed intruder states, "No, neighbors may hear the gun shots."

There's no automobiles parked in the driveway except Cuz's. The next door neighbor Miss Fran, a short pudgy widow, puffy rose cheeks short greying hair arrives at the door carrying a lemon pie, Jona's favorite, Ringing the doorbell several times, no response, not observing the boat dock she thinks to herself, "They must be out on the boat." One of the intruders looking out of the door peephole watches her disappear, he instantly closes the blinds in the front room. Returning home, Miss Fran begins calling the house, again no answer, she goes about baking more pies and cakes, her past time and listening to her favorite CD's, the "LOMAX" band, plus being nosy. Eventually Mr. Detective stops, just to chat with Jona and Cuz, ringing the bell and knocking loudly, no response.

Cuz's girlfriend, Roberta begins calling the house to remind Cuz she is on her way over to fix a special lunch for everyone, no answer, they must be in the yard she thinks. She goes to the house, rings the bell, no response. She goes to the rear door, knocks loudly, nothing.

The boats are at the dock. Her concerns begin to grow. If something came up Cuz would have called her. She returns home, begins calling periodically, and gets a busy signal, strange she thinks to herself; Cuz never talks long on the phone. The intruders, tired of the phone ringing have taken it off the hook.

From time to time the intruders leave Jona and Cuz, go to the kitchen for snacks and a beer or few shots of whisky. During this time Blanket appears, begins clawing and pulling on Cuz's tied ropes. This occurs when the opportunity presents itself.

Cuz is constantly thinking in the back of his mind, if Blanket loosens the ropes enough for him to get his hands free, what could he possibly do? He could go to the exercise room; his weapon could be weights or a weight bar but these are no weapons against a gun. He thinks, devise some sort of scheme or plan if by chance he gets loose.

Eventually he frees himself while the intruders are in the kitchen, quietly opens the door and let's Blanket out. He enters the kitchen, hands above his head, informs the intruders he is ready to compromise, giving them the combination to the safe if they leave and don't harm him or Jona.

It is agreed upon. Opening the safe there is approximately four hundred dollars and some personal papers. The intruders are extremely disappointed and ticked off. Meanwhile Blanket is furiously barking at Miss Fran's door. Miss Fran lets him in. Barking and running in circles, pawing at her legs she senses something is wrong next door, this has never happened before. Roberta has gone to the police station seeking Mr. Detective, she had been introduced to him before by Cuz at the awards ceremony.

Jona is struggling and crying profusely, looking at Cuz's bleeding nose and cut lip. Meanwhile Roberta is informing Mr. Detective how strange it is she hasn't received a phone call from Cuz. Mr. Detective, by habit in deep thought is scratching the back of his head, what should he do? Come up with a plan! Maybe they have been overcome by carbon dioxide, "no," bad thought both, cars are in the driveway, however the phone stays busy! Meanwhile Miss Fran calls the police station while Roberta is there. Mr. Detective instinctively believes this is cause for great alarm. Blanket is Okay, he informs Roberta.

The intruders begin collecting items they believe have some value and placing them in large garbage bags. Cuz's mind is becoming tired and confused from the pain and stress, still he doesn't give up. The reason, unbeknown to anyone, not Jona or Roberta is that Cuz is an entrepreneur, legally and secretively dealing in jewels, diamonds, gems and gold. Several times a year he travels to other countries manipulating business deals. The safe in his closet is for the convenience of petty cash. There is a floor safe just below the floorboards in one of the upstairs bedrooms camouflaged by an expensive oriental rug with an elaborate table over it. In that safe is more than six million dollars' worth of cash, diamonds, gems and expensive collectables. This is one of the reasons he has been so stubborn refusing to cooperate with the intruders.

Saturday becomes Sunday, the scheme is to make a deal with the intruders. He informs them he has a trust fund in the bank worth over thirty thousand dollars in cash and stock certificates, he will give it to them for he and Jona's safety. Jona will remain their hostage, actually, Cuz has over two million dollars in various cash, funds and gems in the bank. He'll go to the bank, return, park across the road, and drop the visible packets of money from the driver's side window. When Jona is released, he will drive off. The intruders are elated at this plan, thinking they've struck gold.

Mr. Detective's plan is to set up inconspicuous plainclothes units in the area observing any activity starting Sunday night through Monday. Monday morning, they observe Cuz enter his car, one car follows him to the bank, he returns to his car. Another officer inquires of the bank official what has transpired! He tells the officer about a very large withdrawal. This information is conveyed to the surveillance units. Cuz unaware returns, drops half of the money as planned. Jona is released, Cuz drops the other half of the money. Cuz and Jona are extremely relieved, but where's Blanket?

The intruders retrieve the money placing it in the garbage bags along with other items of value, run on foot into a nearby wooded area off the roadside. The surveillance team cannot enter the area in their vehicles, they lose track of the intruders. Miss Fran being nosy feels something is wrong, she opens the door, notices one of Cuz's cars is missing, Blanket runs out.

Mr. Detective, exiting his car retrieves Blanket, takes him to the money drop. Blanket excitingly sniffing and barking proceeds into the woods. Mr. Detective, knowing Blanket by now orders the other officers to circle and secure the wooded area, he and his partner on foot follow Blanket. He leads them to a small cleared area where they observe the two intruders sitting outside a truck joyfully smoking weed drinking whisky retrieved from Cuz's house and counting money, he calls for assistance. Upon arrival, they confront and arrest the two suspects without resistance. They are Earl Baker, wanted for Grand Theft and parole violation. His accomplice is David Watson, a convicted felon, served time for Aggravated Robbery. They are charged with robbery, hostage taking and extortion, conviction in court. The other home robberies are included, "cases closed."

They all proceed to Cuz's house where Jona, Cuz and Blanket are reunited. A very happy ending for all. Another joyful celebration. Blanket seems to know, "A Job well done."

"A Boy and His Dog"

Paquita and Bob and Gracie

"SCHOOL DAYS"

Cuz enrolls Jona in an exclusive accredited private school, Jona prefers walking with Blanket rather than taking the bus, Blanket accompanies him each day. While Jona is in school Blanket romps the school grounds not disturbing anyone. Somehow he becomes accustom to the timing of each school bell, the last bell he resigns himself to a special secluded area of the school yard waiting for Jona, they walk home together.

The retreat home is always a pleasant one as they pass and wave to neighbors along the way, the neighbors become accustom to Blanket and Jona. At one house bordered by a white picket fence, there is often a four or five-year-old girl playing in the yard, her name is Cathy. As she sticks her hand through the slats in the fence Blanket prancing along with her on his hind legs is licking her fingers, this is joyful to both of them. It is pleasing to her mother usually sitting on the porch.

One day on their walk from school approaching Cathy's house expecting their few moments of joy together there are numerous police cars, people with cameras, everyone is separated by yellow police tape on each side of the walkway. As Mr. Detective emerges from the house, Jona breaks towards him, "Mr. Detective, what's wrong?" "The little girl that lives here, Cathy, is missing, do you know her?" "Sorta," is Jona's reply? "Well you better go on home, no wait, can I borrow Blanket for a minute?" "Sure." Mr. Detective has an absurd idea, perhaps, just perhaps Blanket can trace Cathy's trail. He picks Blanket up, carries him up the walk to the doorstep. He asks Cathy's mother to give him an article of Cathy's clothing, he puts it in front of Blanket, after all, Blanket has been playing with Cathy, licking her fingers along the fence.

As soon as Blanket sniffs the clothing he jumps from Mr. Detective's arms and runs down the walkway to the curb and immediately stops, dead end. Blanket running in circles at the curb, sniffing and seeming puzzled, Mr. Detective induces, something is wrong here.

Continuing home Jona's heart is sunken, he thinks to himself, "Will my life always be a mixture of happiness and then sadness?" Blanket can sense Jona's mood, he too is not happy, walking slowly behind Jona with his head down. Arriving home, Jona informs Cuz of their experience. Cuz has a quite serious talk with Jona. They discuss the walk home from school, Cuz is also wondering what might have happened to Cathy. An extensive interview with Cathy's mother reveals she was on the porch watching Cathy play, went to answer the phone, conversed for a moment, heard the bells of an ice crème truck or wagon, when she returned to the porch Cathy was gone.

However, she informs Mr. Detective, Cathy was fascinated by the periodic appearance and the bells of ice cream trucks. She recalls, while on the phone she heard bells like that of an ice cream truck and saw one pulling away as she returned to the porch. Mr. Detective, "Can you describe it?" Hysterical, crying, collapsing to her knees, Mr. Detective embraces her. "I know this is hard for you." "Yeah, huh, oh God, my Cathy, the ice cream truck, find her, my Cathy. Please, please, oh, oh, my God, van, truck, no, step van, you know, you know, white, it was white." This gives Mr. Detective some hope towards his investigation.

Immediately a search party is initiated and organized, picture posters are put up, community residents are seriously involved, however, results are negative. The FBI and other authorities become involved. After two days, there is no ransom request.

As expected Cathy's parents are in a state of shock, disbelief and terrified. Cuz runs into Mr. Detective in the grocery store, he informs Cuz about the status of his investigation.

The local owner of an ice cream truck is interviewed, takes a polygraph test, passes it, he proves from witnesses he was on a different route the day and time Cathy went missing. They can find no other owners of an ice cream truck in the area, disappointment and frustration set in. News media with articles and TV broadcast flood the tri state area. A detective Brandson, in the small hamlet of Madisonville becomes aware of Cathy's disappearance, a seven-year-old boy was abducted in his town. He believes this is no coincidence.

He calls Mr. Detective, informs him of what has happened in his nearby town of Madisonville, however no one recalls ever seeing an ice cream truck there. Upon request, they both agree to meet. The important thing is that there was an ice cream truck (van) seen there on the exact day of the young boy, Johnny's disappearance. Witnesses who saw it gave the same description as Cathy's mother. The two towns are only several miles apart. "Bingo" again, something to go on, they have their first meeting, trading information.

After several meetings, Mr. Detective becomes bored with the drive to Madisonville, he asks Cuz if Jona and Blanket could accompany him, Cuz gives his consent. Mr. Detective driving along the way stops frequently purchasing hot dogs, soda and a snack for Blanket. Everyone enjoys the trip.

Meeting with the Madisonville detective, they walk the small narrow sidewalks again showing photos, questioning shop owners and residents.

Jona is helpful pasting up picture posters of Cathy and Johnny he likes this task of being helpful. As they pass a small variety/grocery store. A somewhat elderly couple is putting groceries and toys into a plain white step-van.

The side door is open on the side next to the sidewalk, as they pass the van Blanket jumps in and onto the middle rear seat, sniffing, growling and barking, again disobeying Jona's retrieval command. "Come Blanket, come." Jona repeating himself. Jona is embarrassed and apologies to the couple.

Mr. Detective by now, very familiar with Blanket's behavior, his instincts kick in. "Something is wrong." He informs the others to continue walking in a normal fashion. Not understanding, Blanket turns and runs back to the van barking, Jona has to physically restrain him. Their car is parked some distance away, no chance to follow the couple. Discretely they obtain the license plate number. Seems Jona and Blanket are getting to become junior detectives.

Back at the station, they identify the owner of the van. Mr. Detective informs the Madisonville detective of his past scenarios' involving Blanket and Jona, he is very impressed. He believes Mr. Detective although it seems somewhat of a fairy tale. Now it's time to decide on a workable investigative plan.

The owner of the step-van is Norman Wells, no police record. At this point Mr. Detective realizes he must remain in Madisonville at least two or three days, he calls Cuz and informs him of the situation and that Jona and Blanket are welcome to stay at the detective's home, he has two kids about Jona's age. Cuz agrees no problem. "I'd like to drive down, Okay." "Fine, great, Okay."

Staking out the house of Mr. Wells, the detectives observe no activity the first day. The second day they observe two kids playing Frisbee in the yard, a small girl and a young older boy.

Mr. Detective from a distance believes the girl to be Cathy, he has only seen her picture on posters, and the boy fits the description of Johnny, the other missing child. Now it's time to take action. Based on the information they present to the judge, they are granted a search warrant. The two detectives along with a deputy approach the house to serve the warrant. Inside they find no children, toys or children's clothing. Mr. Detective requests the deputy to retrieve Blanket and Jona from the car.

Approaching the house, Blanket immediately starts running around the yard sniffing and barking. "Stupid idea" the Sherriff thinks to himself. Entering the house again, Blanket is running down the hall from room to room then to the rear kitchen door where he is scratching and barking at the door. Cuz opens the door, Blanket rushes out towards a small makeshift barn, beneath it they find a small cellar, it is decorated as a children's room, posters on the wall, video games, TV, bathing facilities and makeshift bedding. "No children", Cuz thinks, "Why all this? Two kids playing in the yard! Who were they?"

Puzzled they think, "No children!" What's going on here? As they exit the cellar, Blanket rapidly runs to the edge of a wooded area running back and forth, sniffing and whining. Cuz states to the Sheriff, "Oh he just loves to chase rabbits." Walking back towards the house frustration and disappointment sets in, Blanket does not follow them. The Sheriff, referring to Blanket calls, "Come on Police Dog." Jona immediately and angrily responds, "That's not his name, his name is Blanket." Jona informs the Sheriff, "Never call him any other name, he likes his name."

It's agreeable and never happens again. Jona trying to recall Blanket but he doesn't respond. Cuz's curiosity begins to take hold. He tells the Sheriff, "Let's see what's up!"

The three of them approach Blanket, he takes off into the woods, there they find a small utility house, a pad lock on the door. Blanket is digging and scratching in the dirt at the entrance. Bewildered they loudly holler, "Is anyone in there"? The response is a loud cry, "Yes, Yes, Yes, let us out." It is the voices of two young children. Excited, amazed, and extremely happy, they all scream, "Hold on we'll get you out." They have nothing to bust the lock. Jona screams, "Cathy, is that you?" Cathy crying replies, "Hu, Huh, Hu, Huh, please, please help."

The Sheriff radios the Deputy still at the house to find some sort of tool to bust a lock. The couple overhearing the call panics. As the Deputy begins searching the kitchen for some sort of tool, the couple flees the house. Due to the fact, the Sheriff and Deputy's car have blocked the narrow driveway their only means of escape is on foot. The Deputy searching the garage finds a hammer, axe and several other tools, quickly he responds to the Sheriff. They bust the lock on the door, enter, emotions high they are embracing each other, tears flowing down everyone's cheeks. Cathy and her new friend Johnny are rescued.

A happy joyful reunion, everyone hugging, crying laughing and kissing, Blanket, jumping pawing and licking. Returning to the house, they discover the couple has fled. Their joy and happiness takes priority over immediate pursuit of the fleeing couple. First thing is to notify the children's parents. Second, put out an "ALL POINTS BROADCAST." The children after a medical exam are fine, well-nourished and no signs of abuse.

"GREAT NEWS"

Other than the children being rescued, a couple of weeks later the "FBI" notifies everyone the couple has been arrested and charged with kidnapping, fraud and other charges. They have cleared other cases. Their investigation revealed fraudulent adoption papers, photos of other kidnapped children that have been returned to their biological family.

All the witnesses testify there's a conviction on all counts; other children have been rescued because of a gifted dog and exceptional police work. By the way, the special hiking place where Blanket was digging we found the remains of a small animal.

Cuz has a serious talk with Jona, he explains the reasons and rules of adoption. He tells Jona how much he has grown to love him and Blanket and wants to protect their relationship; he knows he can never take the place of his parents. Jona understands and is elated at the news. Cuz initiates the legal process.

Cuz begins planning a wonderful vacation for himself, Jona, Roberta and of course Blanket.

It would be a great and exciting road trip, very scenic. Cuz will never fly! He never talks to anyone about his own family tragedy, he lost his parents in a private plane crash. He deeply emphasizes with Jona's tragedy within himself. He discovers a wonderful resort that offers more than anyone could wish for, boating, fishing, hiking, which they all love, historic sites great shopping and restaurants. Everyone's expectations are rapidly growing. Naturally, they can't wait. The road trip is very enjoyable, wonderful stops along the way.

"KINSHIP - LOVE - MARRIAGE"

Cuz sits Jona down for a serious talk. The conversation is about their biological kinship and Cuz's upcoming wedding. Your father and I were first cousins, though we knew it, sorrowfully, we never met. You and I have the same last name. Our fathers' owned a business together. I was too young to know what actually happened, just stories! There was some sort of disagreement over some business issues and they split up.

My father kept the business, profit wise it had phenomenal growth. Both of my parents died. I was left with an extremely large inheritance, that's why I don't have to work, I'm rich. Do you sort of understand? "Yes sir Cuz." Your father and I because we never met had no way of having ill feelings towards one another.

Next thing Cuz states, "Adoption!" Do you know what that is? "Sorta", Jona replies. Cuz explains. Cuz says, I didn't tell you because I wanted everything to be in order, Okay. "Really, Really, Really," Jona hugging and kissing Cuz, he begins to form tears. Jona understands no one could ever replace his parents but knows he would want to be adopted by Cuz more than anyone in this whole wide, wide world. "Blanket, Blanket, did you hear that?" Blanket happily barking as though he understands. "Of course" Cuz states, "Blanket is a part of our deal."

Next thing, I would never want to take your father's place, I like being Cuz. Now let's discuss this. Roberta would be like your Mother but not a real Mother, more like a Big Sister. "I like it even more" states Jona, "We all love each other anyway."

"THE WEDDING"

Roberta is from a middle class family, very educated, extremely pretty! Brown skinned, hazel eyes, shiny short black hair with a curled bang over her forehead, very well built, deep dimples exposed with the slightest smile exposing her very evenly white teeth. Personality plus, owner of her own insurance agency.

Cuz is taking care of all the wedding expenses, sparing no cost, "Royalty Like," he visions to himself. Cuz has many friends, but has not yet chose a best man, don't ask until you think more about it, he thinks to himself. The wedding is set for spring in his palatial yard overlooking the beautiful lake.

He has planned to have the landscape embroidered with hundreds of flowers of assorted colors. He will build a gazebo for the wedding alter. "Black Tie Affair", a band and orchestra. The fabulous Bernetta McMillan, a well-known celebrity has accepted the invitation to be the soloist. More than 200 invitations have been sent out.

Each of the wedding party's attire, picked by Roberta will be personally tailored. More than ten thousand dollars is allotted to her choice for the bridal gown plus accessories. To Jona and Blanket, "What's all this excitement about, just an old wedding?"

On the other hand, Cuz is tangled up within himself. He thinks, "Oh, oh boy, what's going on? Get it together, chill!" Weeks go by, Cuz realizes he has not chosen a best man.

He thinks to himself, "Anyone will do." Cuz has never before been rattled to this point except the one occasion of his house robbery. He is nervously worried and excited.

The day of the wedding he is befuddled trying to remember where he put the wedding ring he has looked at every day for weeks. Hours become minutes to count down time. "Jona", he screams throughout the house. "Yes sir", Jona mannerly replies. Cuz, "Where's the ring, where's the ring?" "In your pocket Cuz." "Here take it you're the Best Man, let's go."

Coming down the aisle, Roberta is not extremely pretty but more beautiful than ever. Walking the aisle in her beautiful wedding gown with a long train, Blanket at the end prancing behind with the train in his mouth, showing off. The ceremony is preformed, the "KISS." One happy family is carved into the lives of all.

"SNOW BOUND"

Blanket has become a somewhat renowned K-9 celebrity and hero in a large extended area. Media reports, TV appearances with Jona and Cuz. Blanket has gained an abundance of fanfare. (He doesn't understand) but he loves it judged by his active response, barking, jumping and prancing in circles yet displaying disciplined behavior. Jona and Cuz react to all of this media attention in a calm, cool manner.

After all, of this exposure, Cuz begins to receive request from several law enforcement agencies for Blanket's assistance in possibly solving some open unsolved cases. Cuz is advised there are large monetary rewards for anyone leading to the arrest of anyone in these cases.

Cuz knowing he would not need the money, but if any of the challenges were successful, the rewards would go to Jona, adding to the trust fund and inheritance Cuz has secretively arranged for him. Cuz considers all of the consequences, positive vs. negative. School is in summer break. All expenses, travel, lodging, food, even any brief recreation would have to be declared in advance or as it accrued by the requesting agency. A second thought, he does not want Blanket's achievements to this point be tarnished by failure. The final decision will be left to Jona.

Cuz discusses the situation and request for help with Jona. He informs Jona it is his decision, and what the ramifications might be. Jona, a twelve-year-old is confused at such decision-making, it begins to ponder his mind. Cuz has told him to take his time and think about it. Jona, thinking to himself, "Blanket is not a police dog, he's my dog, he's my best friend. But if we can help someone! "Help, help is a good word." People have helped me Blanket and Three Legs, maybe we can help others. I'll talk and explain it to Blanket, if he barks "Okay" happily, we'll try it. These words coming from a twelve-year-old inspires Cuz and again makes him very proud of Jona and his concern for others.

After reviewing several requests, one intensely penetrates Jona's mind. A young girl sledging with her parents disappears in an unexpected snow slide. Jona's mind immediately reverts to his tragic rescue and experience in the cold wintery snow. "Brrr." He shivers, retracing memories to himself. "Oooh, darn winter snow."

He thinks about Three Legs every day. "How is he now, what's he doing, is he safe? I know he remembers us!" A prayer in his thoughts every day, "Three Legs, we love you, hope you're Okay, love you always, GOD bless you." "Brrr again."

The only reluctance Jona has is the remembrance of the devastating cold, snowy wintery weather due to the previous experience he suffered. After further contemplation, he'll accept the challenge, hopefully to rescue or save a young girl's life.

Arriving at the small town ski resort, "Winter Wonder," Jona becomes terrified by past memories but doesn't display it. Shivering within himself, again he thinks, "Cold, horrible snowy weather, I hate it."

Immediately the Sheriff organizes a recall of all the participants that have been involved in the rescue efforts. An "After Report" is communicated to Jona and Cuz about the negative results, also a map of the geographical terrain. Jona thinks, "Wow, I wish Three Legs was here, he knows how to find caves and overhangs."

Weather reports inform them no further snow is expected for several days, that's the good news.

It has only been thirteen hours since, fourteen-year-old Rikki's disappearance.

Jona recalls Mr. Detective requesting an article of Cathy's clothing for Blanket to smell for a scent. He requested an article of Rikki's clothing, preferably, the last night clothing she wore, this would have a stronger scent. Jona is becoming quite a Jr. Detective. Jona and Cuz are given a dual person snowmobile, radio, snowshoes, batteries, every piece of equipment necessary for the elements. Blanket's attire, a bright red hand knitted sweater, which takes him a while to get use to.

Rikki's parents Ray and Denise direct them to the area of the mishap. The search party has previously shoveled into several snow banks to no avail. There are no signs of any tracks in the snow. The rescue to most seems doubtful.

Jona is driving because of his vast experience in this type of weather. Blanket is on his lap. They curiously search around the site, nothing! No snow tracks, no footprints. The sun is out, the snow has been melting, if there were any tracks they may have melted. Disappointment, thoughts of failure sit in.

They begin circling the area of Rikki's disappearance, no success. Jona thinks, if this were him trying to survive he would travel down the slope, not up. They change their search into an up and downhill pattern rather than a lateral one. After several hours of succumbing to the freezing elements they briefly return to town to rejuvenate themselves with warmth, nutrition, hot drinks, tea, coffee, cocoa and energy bars.

They return to the area and continue the search widening the pattern. Maybe the wind has shifted the snow, with no landmarks perhaps the parents were mistaken about the area of disappearance. Blanket has been sitting on Jona's lap on top of Rikki's bed clothing constantly sniffing her scent.

Suddenly, off to the side of their newly changed pattern they observe an unusually wide deep print in the snow, somewhat like that of an elongated ball of snow. Cuz yells for Jona to stop. All three exiting the snowmobile, Blanket sniffing around begins barking. He runs down the steep side of the slope to a small area of sparsely scattered pine trees. Jona and Cuz follow the elongated roll of snow, which has been stopped by the trunk of one of the trees.

Blanket is scratching and barking removing the thick layer of snow, they observe clothing. All three scratching and pawing are screaming, "Rikki, Rikki, is that you?" No response.

She's frozen to death they think. Uncovering Rikki's face, it has turned pale blue, she can't open her eyelids, ice has frozen them together, along with her lips, she can't talk, her toes are frost bitten. Immediately Cuz calls "911", he reports the recovery and that Rikki's barely alive. Cuz request a rescue helicopter.

Receiving the report Rikki's parents are not only in disbelief but shock and happiness at the same time. Rikki is flown to the hospital examined and treated for frostbite and hypothermia, she's in critical condition in the Intensive Care Unit. Family visitors only. Jona, Blanket and Cuz stay overnight to see when they can visit. They are heroes again. The town has been smothered by media for two days, Jona, Cuz and Blanket take it in stride. The next day visitation is allowed to Blanket, Jona and Cuz.

Rikki receives a kiss on each cheek and mouth lickings by Blanket, an engraved bracelet with her name on it, on the underside are three more names! Rikki's parents inform Cuz to go to the bank and receive the reward money, he refuses stating, "Rikki's life is our reward, and we've made a new friend."

A few weeks later, Jona, and Cuz receive a letter with Blanket's name on it also, they read it to Blanket, does he understand? The letter informs them Rikki has made an almost full recovery, attached to the letter is a check for an extremely large amount, the reward money.

What's Next?

"JAMAICA MON"

No Problem

After the extra ordinary exposure from the snow bound incident Cuz's home is overwhelmed with more media, letters, request and even an offer for a book and movie contract. Cuz decides to avoid all of this response and invasion, another Get-a-way for the foursome would be great. Jona is out of school, one of Cuz's favorite vacation spots is in the Caribbean, Jamaica. He begins the process, passports for Jona and Roberta, inoculations for Blanket if necessary. He pulls strings to leave almost immediately. Everyone is happy nervously scurrying about, never being out of the country before. Since Cuz won't fly, he'll rent a chauffeur for the drive to Florida and take a charter yacht to Jamaica where he has made arrangements with one of his International Business friends to use his private fabulous villa and yacht on a small-secluded island, Shangri-La; this would eradicate all of the unwanted fanfare. Cuz has certified Captain's license.

After more than an exciting land trip, they take a small boat to the island from Montego Bay (Mo Bay). Approaching the island, Cuz points out the fabulous villa atop a small cliff, the yacht and private beach. The villa has five bedrooms, whirlpool, large family room, swimming pool, Jacuzzi, tiled flooring, cathedral ceilings on each floor and balconies galore overlooking the Caribbean and a spiral staircase. "Wow," Jona, exclaims, "I'll get lost in here." There are two small boats secured to the dock along with the yacht, beautiful colored flowers and greenery abound among assorted fruit trees and a private swimming pool. It is beyond Jona and Roberta's dreams.

"Fabulous, magnificent" Roberta screams, "I love it already", "Cool Cuz, really cool", Jona shouts. Blanket doesn't know what's going on but he's jumping and dancing, he senses everyone is happy.

Entering the villa, Roberta is breath taken, again she repeats, "Fabulous, magnificent, I love it." Cuz and Roberta are romantically embracing. Jona and Blanket are excitingly exploring inside and outside. There is an abundance of food, drinks, snacks and food for Blanket. Cuz ask, "Is two weeks enough?" "Yes, yes, yes," is their reply. Cuz informs them there are only four other villas on the island and twenty-four-hour security. He also tells them there will be two maids, a cook and gardener arriving in the morning; they will be living in the two cottages on the grounds. No one is accustom to this sort of life with the exception of Cuz.

During supper, Cuz informs them about the history and life style of the people on the main island, Montego Bay. There are no motorized vehicles on Shangri-La, just bicycles, no TV only a radio for news and music plus his cell phone. "That's awesome" Roberta states, "I'm loving it." Jonas only concern is where the bikes are! Cuz tells them of his plans, rafting on the smooth narrow river the "Marta Rae", a log raft made by the natives, shopping, hiking, snorkeling, and most of all spending some days and nights on the yacht. "Gosh, I'll never go to bed", says Jona. Cuz informs them they'll have a native music combo on the verandah some nights.

"There'll never ever be anything to top this," Jona and Roberta think to themselves.

Cuz excuses himself, to make some business calls. Jona, liking to give people nicknames, like "Cuz, Mr. Detective", ask Roberta, "Miss Roberta, what's your last name?" "Jenkins," she replies. "Can I call you R.J?" Roberta says, "Okay, I like it, in fact, I really like it." Jona is pleased. She's become sort of a mother/sister to him.

Cuz returns, after observing the bright moon and stars briefly, everyone retires until early morning anxious for whatever excitement and adventures await them.

The help arrives and are given instructions, a lunch is prepared, and they are off on the yacht to cruise the crystal clear blue and green waters. Cuz gives them a brief tour, explaining the mechanics of sailing. R.J. arms outstretched, twirling in circles, looking towards the sky exclaims, "This is truly heaven". They anchor in a quite lagoon for a swim and lunch, even Blanket enjoys the warm water, he loves sitting on the bow curiously observing the coastline. Continuing, Cuz points out historical landmarks; anchoring off a small village they take a dingy ashore. They experience appetizers, Salt fish and Ackee, Conch, Curried Goat, all of which is different and delicious. The Jamaicans are so delightful and hospitable.

After a first full day of bewilderment, they return to the villa for supper and relaxation. Everyone establishes a rapport with the help, Blanket, especially with the cook who sneaks him a snack or two each day. After a delicious exotic supper Jona retrieves the bike, he and Blanket do more exploring. The Jamaican sunset provides a romantic stroll for Cuz and R.J. through the beautiful flowered garden with hugs and kisses. Back on the verandah, their favorite spot they have wine, hors d'oeuvres, punch and fruit. Time to retire; flowers have been displayed in each bedroom for aroma at night and color in the morning sunlight.

Everyone is up before breakfast, Jona and Blanket are already in the pool before breakfast, afterward they all board the shiny "Christ Craft" speed boat and ride to Mo Bay to meet (longtime friend of Cuz, his island family) Ted a large very dark skinned Jamaican, very white even teeth, smiling with greetings, introduces himself to Jona and R.J.

They're escorted to Ted's wife, Jeneen's seamstress shop; R.J. selects numerous patterns of material and is fitted for native style dresses and head wraps exclusively designed for her; along with hand crafted sandals, and accessories.

They proceed to the "Marta Rae" river for a rafting trip on the calm shallow quite river. The raft is made of small wooden logs secured by ropes and wooden benches attached. The guide has a long wood pole for navigation. Scenery along the way is unimaginable. Jona and R.J. are in all! Blanket is barking intermittently as though he sees something along the shoreline. Almost no words are spoken. Everyone is overtaken by the adventure.

After a stop for lunch, they return to "Mo Bay." Six garments are awaiting R.J., they proceed to town to shop, a very crowded area, Blanket is very much confused but well behaved. Afterward they visit a large open tree house for appetizers and native punches. They return to the villa, a swim and relaxation before supper. R.J. produces her own fashion show for entertainment, displaying each of the dresses Jeneen has made for her. After supper, they relax around the pool, a dip now and then, talking, joking and reminiscing about the adventures of the day. Jona and R.J. are in wonderland.

While Cuz excuses himself, Jona and R.J. have a wonderful conversation getting more acquainted with each other. Blanket is tugging and rolling around in a small blanket Cuz has given him, Jona and R.J. are laughing, amused at his antics. Cuz returns and informs them, "A busy day tomorrow, night, night."

The next day they adventure to and climb "Dunn River Falls," they encounter many more adventures on their Get-a-Way. Overnights on the yacht, fishing, hiking, snorkeling etc. Before they realize it, they're homeward bound.

Arriving home, they find an abundance of request and fanfare has stacked up. R.J. has to return to her insurance agency. Jona and Blanket are trying to readjust.

"ONE HAPPY FAMILY"

Déjà vu

Going through the backed up mail Cuz finds a large white envelope, stamped, "OFFICIAL NOTICE", excited and inquisitive he rapidly tears it open thinking, "What is this?"

It Reads:

> "Your process for the adoption of Jona is final and legal; papers have been filed with the Clerk of Courts in the jurisdiction, Mineral County."

Regards,
Commissioner, Aaron Fulcher

P.S. Contact me regarding Jona's future, i.e. inheritance, education, will, etc.

State of South Carolina

Cuz is elated and relieved, he fixes a strong drink, with his hand over his heart there is a shy of peacefulness. He conceals this information at this time, doesn't share it with anyone, he has plans.

He tells R.J. which he also refers to her now that he would like to go dining, just the two of them, it's "Okay."

While dining Cuz states, "I have a question." "What is it?" "R.J., would you consider selling your insurance agency and just taking care of our family?" R.J. surprised, "Gosh Cuz lets discus this at home for a few days." After several discussions, the answer is a definite, a happy, "Yes." Cuz informs her Jona's birthday is coming up, his birth certificate was sent to me in some papers I received, I don't believe he realizes it, maybe he has forgotten. We have to do something big, think about it. All this time I never thought about, birthday. I knew how old he was from the adoption papers. I hadn't paid any attention to the birth date.

Cuss and Jona continue reviewing the backed up mail. There is one request that has an impact on Jona. A picture of a missing boy, Derron, about Jona's age with his dog Champ in a scout uniform. Jona vaguely recalls he might have been a scout at one time, his memory has not yet fully recovered.

The request reads:

> Dear Blanket, Jona and Mr. Cuz, could you please give your assistance, we are trying to find our son, Derron who disappeared on a scout outing, along with his dog Champ. We have seen you in the media, you are our Hope, "God," is our Faith, pray with us.
>
> The Willis Family.

The family lives in Tapie, New Mexico, Jona considers the areas warm climate, that's the good news; the other is his feeling of empathy for Derron and his dog. He would not want He would not want to be separated from Blanket. Cuz informs Jona that they may not always be successful. Its "Okay" is Jona's reply, "We'll do our best." Cuz contacts the Willis family, informs them of all his request, up-front expenses, lodging, equipment, transportation, food, etc. An agreement is finalized. Cuz informs the family there is no guarantee of success.

Upon arrival, a Park Ranger escorts them to the campsite; they interview the Scoutmaster and Derron's tent mate. He informs them Derron lost his pocketknife, he knew where and he would be right back, he and Champ left. Cuz is thinking, he must have gotten disoriented in the dark. If he were attacked by a wild animal, some type of remains would have been found by now. The search has been going on for three days.

The park is typically canyon terrain, very steep cliffs and sparse greenery. The search team is reorganized. The scouts had been told not to venture off without a companion, day or night, this was not the case in this incident. Concerns for Derron's survival are dwindling, despair sets in, thoughts of success diminishing. Jona has procured Derron's sleeping bag for Blanket to get a scent. As the search widens more disappointment sets in. Jona thinks, geographically, "This land is stupid."

As darkness sets in, they retreat to the Ranger's Head Quarters, food and sleep. The Ranger now called "Mr. Ranger" because of Jona provides Cuz with a map of the area including the campsite. This experience is nothing like they have ever encountered before.

Day four, all parties resume the search. Blanket is periodically given a scent of Derron's sleeping bag. Traveling a steep canyon cliff, Blanket runs to its edge barking loudly, his barking sends back a loud "echo," puzzled and frightened he runs to Jona who consoles him. The search party finds it somewhat amusing.

As they walk on, Blanket turns and runs back to the spot but no longer barking he's scratching and pawing in the dirt at the very edge of the cliff. Again, he doesn't respond to Jona's recall.

Cuz and Jona inform Mr. Ranger something is wrong! Returning, they find a freshly broken tree limb; below they observe a small broken branch on a small narrow ledge below. Mr. Ranger summons for other Rangers to meet and assist him for further investigation. The Rangers often train for all type of rescue situations; they are trained rescue experts in this type of terrain.

They secure Mr. Ranger as he repels down the cliff. As he lands on the ledge, he discovers a very small cave opening and a small motionless body. He communicates his findings. Derron is barely breathing, severely dehydrated and speechless. Champ is lying beside him, whining and licking his face. Apparently, he misplaced his footing at the edge of the cliff due to the darkness. A special harness is lowered, Derron is retrieved along with Champ. A helicopter arrives for evacuation. There are solemn tears of joy, clapping and hugging. Derron's parents are notified. Blanket is rewarded with numerous, pats, hugs and even kisses.

At the hospital, everyone is informed Derron will be fine in a couple of days, more clapping, hugs and licking by Blanket. Cuz calls home and informs R.J. of the success, crying she is elated everyone is safe. She prepares a special meal for their return. Now there are "Two Happy Families."

Susan and Apollo

"BIRTHDAY # 13"

A Teenager

R.J. comes up with a great idea, give Jona a surprise birthday party. Not only that, but invite all of the people he, Blanket and Cuz have rescued. Rikki, Cathy, Johnny, Derron and his dog Champ and their families, Mr. Detective, Mr. Ranger, Mr. Sheriff, school friends and neighbors.

They have six bedrooms, motel accommodations for overnighters will be paid for by Cuz, sleeping bags for the kids.

This will take some exciting enjoyable planning. R.J. is taking care of the planning for an array of catering services. Cuz will arrange for live entertainment, boat rental from the marina, rowboats, kayaks and canoes, an outdoor affair, wonderful. The longer they plan the more everything escalates, games, prizes for each kid, clowns, etc. They renege on an ice cream truck because of Cathy's experience.

The plan: Early morning, on Jona's birthday have "Miss (wonderful, nosey) Fran" take Jona to the Zoo. He has never been there before; this will give us time to prepare everything. On the drive, Jona gets tired of listening to "Thomas and the Lomax Band" CD's. Blanket has been left at home. As the plan grows so does everything else, flowers, favors on each table, decorations everything begins to expand. "No Problem Mon." Cuz and R.J. think, "WOW", everything is taken care of, not the case!

The invitations have been delivered, people begin arriving early morning as requested. Suddenly Cuz realizes, no Birthday

Cake. What to do? "Oh hell." Cuz thinks, call Max's Bakery. He informs them of his dilemma, they have two round cakes and three sheet cakes. Please put birthday decorations on all of them, big tip, quick delivery, Okay! The response from the other end of the phone is, "Done." What else R.J.? "Ice cream!" "Darn some ice cream, no truck." Remembering Cathy's ordeal. Cuz calls the bakery again. "Max, I need about ten more sheet cakes. Can you do it?" "No problem Mr. Jason. Everything is a GO."

Miss Fran is called to start home. On the return trip Jona is thinking, please don't play anymore Thomas and the Lomax Band. As they pull into Miss Fran's driveway Jona stares at the vast amount of land at the rear of Cuz's house, bewildered and inquisitively he asked, "What are all those people doing in our back yard?" Miss Fran says, "I don't know let's go see."

As they approach the rear of the house, everyone begins singing, "Happy Birthday", until they sing the phrase, "Happy Birthday Dear Jona." Tears in his eyes he collapses to the ground on his knees covering his face; wiping his tears, embarrassed, happy and smiling at the same time. Blanket, Cuz and R.J. rush to him. Cuz takes him in his arms whispering in his ear, "It's Okay, it's your Birthday, Okay."

With a happy face he begins to recognize everyone, friends, friends he thinks. Hugging and kissing he's extremely happy. Blanket and Cocoa are in their own world playing with each other. Everyone is happy and excited. Jona has an abundance of gifts, however there is one special gift. Cuz and R.J. approach him with a tiny gift-wrapped box, inside Jona finds a bracelet with the name "JONA" engraved on it, on the underside is engraved "Blanket, Cuz, R.J." It's like the one Cuz had given Rikki. The bracelets will always be a remembrance and connection to both of them.

Everyone has had a great time, the overnighters have brunch and more fun the next morning. The parting is bittersweet with tears, hugs and more kisses. Jona thinks, "The Greatest Birthday of All."

"A Boy and His Dog"

"A SHOE AND A SOCK"

Weeks later, relaxing and reflecting on the extraordinary birthday event everyone has returned to peaceful normalcy. Mr. Detective with reluctance approaches Cuz. He really doesn't want to interrupt the family's routine life style at this time but this is the situation! He informs Cuz. A teenage girl, "Jan" has been missing since overnight. She was returning from church choir rehearsal and was dropped off at the family mailbox on the side of the road about thirty yards from her farmhouse.

It had been sprinkling rain, a shoe, umbrella and choir book was found near the mailbox. Tracks in wet trampled grass indicated signs of a dragging struggle. Already an "AMBER ALERT" has been initiated. The National Center for Missing Children and other law enforcement agencies have been notified. A search team is initiated, an intense investigation has begun, because of this vast agrarian area, the National Guard has become involved.

Cuz has immediate concerns for Jan's hopeful rescue and welfare, however he has personal concerns for Jona. How much exposure and possible stress can a now thirteen-year-old endure? Media exposure, book and movie offers, letters of request for rescue assistance. Cuz knows Jona is not daunted by past challenges, he has never failed yet in previous rescue efforts. Cuz realizes the immediacy of the situation. He informs Mr. Detective he needs time to contemplate about the request however, it will be Jona's decision. Blanket is Jona's dog, not his. Cuz has been informed Jan's family is a small struggling farm family, they could not afford compensation for any expenses incurred.

Cuz has a serious conversation with Jona informing him of the family's tragic ordeal. Jona's quick response is, "Okay, let's go." Actually, Cuz knowing Jona is not taken back, he expected a response such as this from Jona. It's a short forty-minute drive to Jan's home. Jona and Blanket love drives in Cuz's cars. Arriving, they get a generous welcome then a briefing of the entire scenario.

The Police Chief of this small farming town has no experience in this type of investigation. Jona, now being a "Jr. Detective" request Jan's shoe, knowing there would be no scent from the choir book or umbrella because of the rain there would be one in the shoe.

Jona gives Blanket the shoe, he has a scent, Jona takes him to the mail box, sniffing he leads them to indentations in the wet grass, the middle indentations reveal dragging and intermittent stomping, on each side are shoe impressions that lead to the road, indications lead to the suspicion at least two individuals are involved.

Jona, Blanket and Cuz join a small group of the search team, about a mile from Jan's house they stop for a break at a small roadside rest area. They search the restrooms, nothing. Blanket is rambling the grounds, suddenly he approaches Jona carrying a sock in his mouth. Jona retrieves the sock, they follow Blanket to a particular spot where he begins barking and scratching at the ground. Cuz states, "Jan has been here." They call for the rest of the search team to meet them, the Chief arrives, he and Cuz exchange information.

The Chief informs Jona and Cuz that during an interview with the next-door farmer who came out to retrieve his tractor from the rain, it was just becoming dark.

He noticed an automobile speeding erratically west on the road. He thought to himself, "Huh, damn drunk, waiting to get arrested." Unknown at this time, Jan was in the back seat struggling with one of the individuals, scratching, kicking and biting. What was unusual, the farmer described the vehicle as a station wagon with wood paneling on the sides, the kind you seldom see anymore.

At Cuz's suggestion, they begin to inspect the two lidded trash containers that luckily have been emptied recently. Inside one of them, they retrieve two empty beer bottles, a water bottle and a discarded Wendy's bag with partial food remains with a receipt inside with a time stamp. These items are turned over to the FBI. Meanwhile the FBI has taken the items to the largest nearby police station to be dusted for prints.

Jona, Cuz, Blanket and the Chief question the employees at Wendy's that were working the night before at the time stamped on the receipt inquiring if any recalled such an order. Luckily, the young man, a car buff working the drive-thru recalled two young scroungy looking male Whites requested the order, he remembered because they were driving an old Ford Station Wagon with side wood panels.

The same description the farmer had given. Meanwhile the FBI is having success, they have two good latent prints, they are processing them for an identity match, which comes through quickly. Both prints are those of William "Billy Bullfrog" Benton, he has an extensive police record, Assault, Domestic Violence, Robbery, Carrying a Concealed Weapon and numerous open traffic warrants.

They have a mug photo and a last known address, which is a trailer park. Inconspicuously driving around the trailer park, they find no station wagon fitting the description. Disappointment sets in. They do not question any of the residents' believing it may tip off the investigation; instead, they place a surveillance team near the park entrance. Bullfrog is at this time only a suspect. The surveillance team has had no success. They begin to think maybe this is a bad address.

Cuz thinks they could be here for days. He has an idea, have Blanket and Jona walk the rows of the trailer park. Jona presents the shoe and sock to Blanket for a fresh scent. After walking numerous rows, finally Blanket runs up a short walkway to a particular trailer sniffing the several steps to the doorway sniffing and scratching at the entrance. Jona retrieves him they return to Cuz, the Chief and the surveillance team. Jona tells them, "I believe Jan is in there or has been there. Its number 43 Birch Walk."

After procuring a search warrant, they forcibly enter the trailer and find Jan unconscious on the bed. They can't awaken her. The Para-Medics arrive, examining Jan, they realize she has been drugged. At the hospital, it is confirmed. The good news is other than bruises and a cut lip she has not been molested. Her parents have been notified of the recue, arriving at the hospital there is a happy tearful reunion. Slowly regaining her senses, from a photo mug shot, she identifies "Bullfrog" as one of her assailants.

The surveillance continues, no luck, it's called off. Area authorities have been notified, the Highway Patrol has stopped the station wagon, made an arrest of the two suspects. The accomplice is one David Weathers, he has scratch marks on one side of his face, imprints of bite marks on his left hand. Apparently, that Jan is one hell of a fighter, "Country Girl."

Cuz immediately calls, R.J. with the good news, they're headed home, and she begins cooking another special meal. Arriving home thy have a happy joyful evening, they relate the venture to R.J. in detail. Blanket gets a special meal, a bunch of petting and hugging.

Days later Cuz receives a call from the FBI informing him the suspects have confessed. Their story was they were intoxicated and committed the crime on a lark. With the abundance of hard evidence, they have no one need to appear in court. This saves Jan the agony of testifying.

"A SPECIAL WEEKEND"

Miss" Wonderful Nosey" Fran visits, no cake or pie, she informs everyone they are invited to her house for supper Saturday. Her daughter Jill, Son-in-Law Wayne and grandson, Charley are visiting for the weekend. Her grandson is Jona's age. "By the way, I don't want to hear of your last rescue adventure. Save it so everyone can hear about and enjoy it at the same time." Everyone is happy for her and themselves. Jona is hoping he doesn't have to listen to "Thomas and the Lomax Band" all evening.

Everyone arrives Friday, they're greeted and have a short period of getting acquainted. Jona and Charley hit it off right away. Jona and Blanket show him around, he has never visited before, only his mother, it's the first visit for the whole family. Jona shows him the game room, Charley is amazed, next, with life jackets, even Blanket has one, they take a short adventure in the rowboat. Cuz, R.J, Carol and Wayne hit it off right away also. R.J. invites everyone for an early brunch the next day and a cruise on the pontoon. Jona has invited Charley to go fishing in the morning, Charley has never fished before.

At the dock, Jona explains the tactics of fishing to Charley, who is thoroughly exited with his very first catch of half dozen bluegills or so. R.J. goes to the dock and takes pictures for Charley to have as keepsakes.

After brunch, everyone goes on the pontoon. Cuz identifies points of interest and its history, they take in the beautiful scenery and calm peacefulness on the blue water. Jona, Blanket and Charley are taken for a fun tube ride. Charley is in a dream world. Carol relates, "It's so breath taking." Returning home, they lounge around the dock Miss Fran is extremely happy for such a wonderful visit, she is happily crying inside.

Jona, Blanket and Charley walk the coves skipping rocks, throwing twigs for Blanket to retrieve. Charley doesn't have a dog, he has fallen in love with Blanket, and he tells Jona he's like another person. Wayne informs Cuz how wonderful the outing was.

Miss Fran has prepared an extraordinary supper, Jona's lemon meringue pie and peach cobbler for desert. After supper Jona, Blanket and Charley are anxious to get to the game room. The adults exchange chitchats over drinks. Miss "Wonderful Nosey" Fran can't wait to hear about Jona, Blanket and Cuz's last rescue mission. Cuz has a great talent as a storyteller though he displays a state of humility unlike when he is conducting business. Cuz begins telling about the rescue. It's all ears, like everyone is reading a great detective novel. (Hand clapping) When Cuz is finished they tell him they actually believed they were there, how exciting.

Sunday it's another early brunch, the ladies fix a lunch for the boat cruise. Jona, Blanket and Charlie are on the dock fishing again, Charley is "hooked", not like a real fish.

They catch several more bluegill, then, "WOW." a large trout, over excited Jona screams, "Get the net, get the net." Charley doesn't know what he's talking about, Charley doesn't know what a net is! Cuz hears the screams, runs to the dock advising Jona how to bring the fish in, Cuz grabs the net and lands the fish, about an eight pounder. R.J. takes more pictures of all of them, she makes copies for Charley.

On the pontoon they anchor for lunch in a lovely cove, Jona, Blanket and Charley go for a swim. The adults have a wonderful conversation laughing and listening to music, everyone has established a wonderful rapport.

Returning to the dock R.J. has a great thought, "Why don't I fix the catch of the day, baked trout." "Wonderful suggestion for supper, fresh out of the water." Says Wayne. Jill, "That would be a wonderful experience for us R.J, let me help."

Near the time for departure, Wayne and Jill near tears, exchange hugs and kisses with Cuz and R.J. Miss Fran is smothered with tears. Wayne tells them they know Charley will never forget this visit, neither will we. Cuz, "We'll do it again soon." Jill, "This has been a Special Weekend."

"DIAMONDS, GEMS AND PARIS"

Due to less media coverage request have somewhat dwindled, Cuz is pleased with this. Mr. Detective visits Cuz in a somewhat humble manner. Cuz ask, Will, which is Mr. Detective's first name, "What's wrong?" Mr. Detective answers, "I need to tell you something." In a surprising reaction, Cuz ask, "What?"

In a monotone, humble voice Mr. Detective responds "Cuz, the girl Jan, you Jona and Blanket rescued was my cousin's niece." "Damn" Cuz states angrily. "Why didn't you tell me?" "I didn't want to influence your decision to respond to the request, we're friends, we're friends." Cuz hugging Mr. Detective softly whispers in his ear, "I can respect that, it's behind us, I'm even happier now, I feel great." Mr. Detective. "Thanks Cuz." "Thanks not necessary, I'm sure Jona will be happy."

As usual, unexpectedly, Cuz's secret associate Ralph Winkler, elderly gentleman, somewhat flamboyant, mid-sixties, silver graying hair, wrinkled face slight build; calls Cuz and informs him they need to be in Paris for a special diamond and gem auction just two weeks away. Cuz immediately books a one-way cruise for himself since he won't fly.

Cuz has his personal driver and part time bodyguard; Marvin Butts, six foot, six inches tall, one hundred and ninety-five pounds, handsome, brown skinned, smokes stogies and is a skilled martial artist, always wears cowboy boots and a hat, and rides a Harley.

Cuz has known Marvin since he was a young kid transporting elderly ladies with their groceries in his "little red wagon" making small change. Marvin is like an adopted son. Now the CEO of a successful air travel, car-detailing service, "Mr. Bubbles / Air Marvin Travel." He and wife Tabatha, extremely attractive, a beauty contest winner and well-known singer manages "Mr. Bubbles." They are always at Cuz's beckoning call. Marvin is also a licensed Private Investigator. He always accompanies Cuz on such business trips.

Cuz's thoughts ponder, he's never been separated from Jona and Blanket before, only R.J. on rare occasions. This is a small dilemma, what to do? This takes some thought and consideration. Suddenly he gets a brainstorm! Arrange for Jona, Blanket and R.J. to fly to France and meet him, there would be plenty of time after the auction to spend time together. Visit the Eiffel Tower, the Luv, Mt. Sac Cracaer (Momarte), Notre Dame, fine French restaurants, etc. Realizing no one would want Blanket to be placed in a kennel. Everyone could fly home afterward, he being the exception.

Cuz is happy and content after a successful auction. He immediately sends most of the purchased stones home to his bank by a special insured courier. He gives a small amount to Ralph to deposit in his home floor safe upon Ralph's return home. This is for immediate access should the need arise. For years, Ralph has been a loyal, trustworthy dedicated associate to Cuz.

A knock on the door to Ralphs's suite, "Who is it?" states Ralph in a loud voice. "Room Service" a voice responds. "You've got the wrong room, I didn't request Room Service," opening the door two males wielding a service cart and pistols demanding the gems Cuz has given him. Ralph informs them he doesn't have any gems.

They begin beating him severely, he gives them the combination to the hotel room safe, its contents are approximately $4000.00 a passport, Rolex watch, credit cards and an inexpensive diamond ring and auction receipts. After gagging Ralph and tying him to the bedpost, they ransack the suite and leave.

Everyone has had a fantastic time sightseeing and dining. Returning to the hotel, Cuz begins calling Ralph's suite, no answer. Cuz becomes irritable, agitated, Jona and R.J, have never seen him in this state of mind. He examines the hotel premises, lounge, exercise room, no Ralph. The Door Man recalls Ralph arriving but never leaving. Cuz becomes increasingly alarmed. He demands the Manager access Ralph's suite, entering everyone is shocked beyond belief observing the unbelievable horrible state Ralph is in, he's bloody from being beaten, restrained and incoherent, the suite is in shambles.

Cuz's mind reflects to his own encounter with the intruders. The Police and Medics arrive, Ralph is transported to the hospital immediately. Cuz is interviewed and gives them all the information he can. He is devastated observing Ralph in such a horrible state. The investigators trying to procure information are confronted with a slight language barrier, which does not help the investigation. Cuz's concern is Ralph. Jona and Blanket are allowed to enter the marked off crime scene, Blanket, sniffing around runs to the elevator door then to the concrete stairwell exit, dead-end. Cuz leaves immediately for the hospital.

Ralph is diagnosed in serious, almost critical condition, incoherent, broken whispered speech that Cuz can make nothing but nonsense of, neither can the police. At Ralph's bedside Cuz is attempting to comfort Ralph and shows his concern. Ralph is twelve years Cuz's senior but in good health, he had previously worked for Cuz's father and could be trusted.

That's one of Cuz's many likeable traits about Ralph. Cuz is at his bedside consoling him. Ralph barely conscious whispers to Cuz. "Ice, ice." Cuz summons the nurse requesting a cup of ice; she brings it, Cuz handing the cup to Ralph who shakes his head "No" waving the cup away.

Cuz is confused, Ralph a few seconds later points to the water pitcher on his bed table, Cuz gets it, Ralph shaking his head negatively barely waves it off. Cuz is dumbfounded, thinks this is a game of charades. Ralph returns to unconsciousness due to the medication. Cuz leaves returning to the crime scene where the investigators have accomplished nothing.

Cuz's brain is scattered with thoughts of Ralph's erratic short whispering sentences during their conversation. He thinks, "Ralph is out of it." He tries to dismiss his mind's recollection of the visit but it lingers.

At the crime scene investigators request Cuz to go through all of Ralph's belongings, nothing of interest, all monies and personal papers are missing, passport, everything. Cuz, scratching his head, for some unknown reason focuses on a glass and pitcher partially filled with water and melting ice. Perhaps it has something to do with the broken mumbling conversation he had with Ralph. Walking over to the pitcher he picks it up along with the glass, peering down to pour himself a glass of water; he's struck by a blurred assortment of colors at the bottom of the pitcher, emptying the contents everyone is amazed at what is exposed. Besides water there's a clear plastic "Glad" sandwich bag containing the gems he had given to Ralph in private. Staring at each other, smiling with soft giggles. Cuz states, "That screwed ass SOB" referring to Ralph. But how could someone know? "Surveillance cameras," one of the investigator's replies, "They're in all auctions of this sort, possibly a security breach."

Cuz, fighting his fear of flying books himself on the flight home. He wants to be at Ralph's side. Cuz is petrified but doesn't display his fear. Arriving home, R.J. is attending Ralph along with a nurse Cuz has hired.

Blanket is relieved he is no longer confined to the caged animal compartment on the plane. Blanket has grown affectionate to Ralph while his wounds are healing. At least once a day he brings a "blanket" from another room and places it at Ralph's bedside, the affection becomes mutual. Possibly, because of the language barrier the robbers have not been apprehended.

Perhaps they never will be.

"TIME FOR SCHOOLING"

Ralph has no family but a girlfriend he didn't want to be notified of the incident until he was in better condition. He always visits Cuz, Jona, Blanket and R.J on occasion for a social visit. Cuz and Ralph are still business associates.

Even though the trip was cut short, Jona and R.J. marveled at the experience. Blanket seems more than happy to be back home. Miss Fran shows up with a lemon pie as an excuse to hear all about the trip, the terrible incident is not discussed. Jona and R.J. are compiling a wonderful scrapbook about all of their get-a-ways, media coverage of their rescues and those rescued. The birthday party, etc.

More and more, requests are dwindling. Cuz reluctantly declines them with Jona's interest in mind.

Movie and book offers are constant. The movie offers are pretty much a definite "NO." Feeling it would be too much pressure on Jona. Book offers require more consideration and future thought.

Recalling the horrible ordeal with the intruders and now this recent incident in Paris, he feels it is necessary to confide in Jona and R.J. about his entrepreneurship and have knowledge of his business. After all, what if something happened to him. "God Forbid." What about the estate and all of his assets not withstanding trust, insurance and wills, etc.? Since the adoption and marriage he has had very extensive concrete papers drawn up, so called, "book ends."

Cuz contemplating for some time realizes he has an obligation to Jona and R.J. to confide in them, after all, they are a family. After supper on a particular evening Cuz feels comfortable, this is the right evening for this type of family dialogue. A knowledge of important family life. Cuz starts with a small extent of "brain washing, "Repeat after me," he says to them confusingly, "There is only one safe in this house." Again, "There is only one safe in this house." Jona and R.J. together repeat the same words. Jona and R.J. thinking to themselves, stunned and stupidly puzzled they don't understand, it's like going around the Mulberry Bush three times. "Okay", Cuz states, "Just remember, there is only one safe in this house." Not all at once Cuz thinks to himself, don't tell them everything at once, tell them bits and pieces.

He begins to inform them about his business, if anyone asks questions, they are to tell them he's only a small investor. He explains what and why things happened to Ralph in Paris. He directs them to follow him to one of the upstairs bedrooms, opening the small safe, which contains some fake personal papers, about two thousand dollars and some worthless zircons and gems. He then directs them to a room down the hallway, moving a large dinner table folding back part of an oriental carpet a trap door that has been installed; beneath lies a large elongated flat safe. Astonished, bug eyed and speechless Jona and R.J. are awed. Cuz does not reveal the combination to this safe at the time, as he has done with the smaller safe.

Cuz retrieves several stones from each safe and they return to the living room fireside. He places the stones separately dividing each small cluster on the table. He hands them a small jeweler's eyeglass and tells them to distinguish each by comparison, some are almost worthless. He informs them the value is in the deepness of color below the surface, as far as diamonds they are valued on what is called the three C's, Color, Cut and Clarity. Jona and R.J. are great listeners and students. Cuz is extremely pleased and relieved about this endeavor through this entire process. Blanket is tilting his head from one side to the other not understanding what's going on. Cuz stands and snaps "Lesson over, more next time, wine and punch, relax."

The next morning Cuz's head is fresh, clear and satisfied that some of the decisions he has been confronted with have been overcome. After breakfast, Cuz suggest Jona invite Miss Fran for a short noon cruise on the boat. Jona and Blanket have a short swim. They have a joyful afternoon laughing and joking about themselves. Returning home, they hug and depart company. Miss Fran, her cheeks covered lightly with tears, she's a cryer, disappears. Cuz, Jona and R.J. feel they have done a good thing, they feel great.

"A TOUCHING REQUEST"

Cuz has an extremely hard task ahead of him, reluctant to accept any more request, this one is heart wrenching and personal. Cuz was born on a mountaintop in West Virginia. There was no nearby hospital. As a family tradition, everyone had to be born in the same family house built by his Great, Great Grandfather Mr. James Jason. Upon his entry into the world, he was given his first taste of water in a spoon by his Great Uncle Aubrey Jason, who was massacred in World War II "The Battle of the Bulge" by German SS Troops.

His brother Robert was blown up on an ammunition war ship both received numerous medals posthumously. His cousin Donald was a prisoner of war for thirty-three months in a North Korean prison camp. His Uncle Bus told him of his involvement in the Battle of the Bulge after the war was over. His Aunt Stella served as a nurse in the war, so did his Uncle Frank Freeman. These were also your relatives. He at the time was very young, he joined the military himself during peacetime.

He was in a very elite outfit, Airborne/Special Forces; he has a very special place in his heart for the military, which will exist forever. Jona is in awe and honored by his family's military history.

The request reads:

Dear Mr. Cuz,

Our son, PFC, Donald Britton training with the 8th Mountain Company on a three, day bivouac disappeared the third day of maneuvers. Because this occurred on a Government Reservation the FBI and Amy are involved in the investigation. It is our hope and prayers you will also respond to aid them, we have heard and read so much about yourself, Jona and Blanket, please help us.

Mr. and Mrs. Ronald Britton

Cuz immediately confronts Jona and informs him of their family's military history, he again tells him all of their missions are not going to be successful. Jona's response as always is, "Let's go." Cuz expected nothing less.

The investigators are still at the bivouac scene when Cuz, Jona and Blanket arrive, they are aware of their past missions and accept them to assist in the investigation and rescue/recovery efforts.

Cuz receives a briefing. The last night of the maneuvers was the last time any anyone in the nine, man squad saw PFC Britton.

He was tented with his buddy Ken Lott, they bunked together for weeks at base camp. Desertion or AWOL are out of the question due to the fact "Ronnie" his nickname had a wedding planned in a couple of weeks before leaving for Afghanistan. Suicide was not even considered, there is no note or body found. The last letters to his parents and fiancée, he informed them how excited he was about the upcoming wedding.

The bivouac area has been searched intensely prior to Jona, Cuz and Blanket's arrival. They are directed to PFC Britton's tent. They are given the above information plus the Platoon

Leader informs them what a good soldier PFC Britton was with potential advancement pending.

The search becomes wider as they enter day two, no positive results, not a trace. Jona now a little more than a Jr. Detective request PFC Britton's sleeping bag, not to disturb anything else. Blanket sniffs both sleeping bags. Somewhat confused he runs to PFC Britton's bunking buddy PFC Ken Lott pulling and sniffing at his pant leg. Jona commands Blanket, "No Blanket, no." Blanket then gets a scent from Britton's sleeping bag, he runs around, not to disturb anything he sniffs both sleeping bags. Again, somewhat confused he runs to bunking buddy PFC Lott pulling and sniffing at his pant leg again. Again Jona commands, "No Blanket, no." There are so many tracks around the area. After several days of disappointment, the thought of failure sets in as it has many times before. The terrain is hard and rocky, very mountainous, some sandy ground. Finally, the helicopters are called off. The army is making arrangements to provide a skeleton search team to continue. While regrouping at the bivouac area preparing to disband the larger search, Blanket who has been roaming the area on his own on returns to Jona with a piece of partially shredded army fatigue material, "Army Issue." This incident immediately commands the entire search team to continue.

Blanket continues to approach PFC Lott scratching and pulling at his pant leg. Lott tells Jona to keep his dog away from him. Jona tells Lott, "He just likes you." One of the FBI agents believes a small stain on the material is blood but is not sure, he wants it taken to forensic ASAP to be tested, if so what type? Blanket meanwhile has not been active; he has not left the bivouac area leading Jona and Cuz to where he found the piece of shredded material.

Again, Blanket runs to PFC Lott scratching at his pant leg, Jona gives a seldom scolding to Blanket, he lies down whining and becomes passive and subdued. Jona and Cuz become puzzled by Blanket's behavior. Everyone reorganizes to resume the search at the orders of the Commander.

Jona and Cuz realize Blanket is not his usual self, they wonder, what is it? The FBI (AIG) Agent In Charge receives the results from the forensic. The stain on the material is blood, but not PFC Britton's, his blood type is "O", the stains are type "AB." This poses a more intensive investigation and search. The Commander and FBI (AIG) order every soldier in Britton's squad to surrender their Dog Tags. Out of the squad of nine, only three have type "AB" blood. PFC Ray Howard, Ken Lott and Dave Bush. The search and investigation intensify. The three soldiers are interviewed. Ken Lott's interview turns into an interrogation due to the fact, his answers to certain questions are not acceptable. He becomes a person of "special interest." The Commander, Cuz and the AIG begin to confer. They believe there are too many things PFC Lott is holding back and not being truthful. The "AIG" suggest the search be restricted to a smaller area, Blanket could not have roamed too far, it's done!

Passing a particular area Blanket runs to a small area of closely scattered large rocks not indicative of the immediate terrain. He begins pawing and barking. Jona states, "There's something there." Beneath the rocks, the ground is soft, smooth and patted down. The Commander orders the rocks be carefully removed. As one-soldier turns a rock over he discovers a red stain, could it be blood? They hope not. Removing the rocks, they find soft dirt. Carefully digging with their hands and fingers in the soft sand like ground, they find a corpse clad in army fatigues. The upper left side of the forehead has been bludgeoned. The "AIG" calls the Forensic Team. The soldiers are ordered to return to the tent bivouac area where they are considered confined to quarters.

Forensic arrives and investigates, the scene is immediately determined a homicide. The stain on one of the rocks is the blood of PFC Britton. Unlike previous rescues, this one does not have a happy ending. Cuz is worried about Jona who seems to be unshaken. There have been too many footprints at the crime scene to be of any help to forensic. Dog tags on the corpse are identified as those of, PFC Britton.

Jona becomes suspicious of why Blanket is always following PFC Lott around and no one else. Everyone returns to base camp. PFC Lott is taken in for more questioning. Being "Government Issue", he is ordered to give a blood sample. Not only does the sample found on the scrap of material Blanket retrieved, but traces of drugs are found in PFC Lott's system. After a lengthy interrogation, PFC Lott confesses to the murder of PFC Britton. His story reveals the events leading to PFC Britton's death.

PFC Lott: "I wasn't on drugs when I entered the army, my first weekend pass I met a girl, we had fun partying; she introduced me to drugs. PFC Britton noticed a change in my behavior, he confronted me and I told him, it's this army life. About two hours before reveille everyone was asleep, he accidentally surprised me at the latrine at the edge of the woods, not intentionally, I had drugs lying on the ground. He said "Damn man, what is this shit?" I told him it was medication. He relieved himself. Later he found out I was hiding drugs in my boot. The last encounter he observed me taking drugs from my sock in my back pack."

On bivouac, laying in our sleeping bags he informed me he was going to report me to our Commander. He said, "I'm not going into combat with a damn druggie." He got up and started walking, I followed him pleading and begging him not to report me. My mind was thinking about a Dishonorable Discharge, even the "Brigg."

Face to face, we had a shoving match. He was adamant about his intensions. I pushed him and he fell. I lost control, picked up a rock and struck him. I went back to our tent got my shovel, buried him and tried to camouflage the grave with rocks. That's when I cut my knee. That damn dog!

After a short military trial, PFC Lott is sentenced twenty-five years to life at Fort Leven Worth. It was a devastating experience for everyone, Jona's thoughts returned to the Randolphs. An unsuccessful rescue for the first time, it turned out to be a sad and tough recovery. There was no celebration, no special supper.

"UNCERTAINTY"

Cuz feels like he has a pebble in his shoe. He realizes there may be ramifications from the last mission. What impact this may have on all of them. He visualizes their exploits turning into a business, sort of like "Bounty Hunters." This thought is not pleasant. Jona is entering high school which will take precedent over all else. From this point on it will not be Jona's decision, but his, if any.

Cuz begins to reluctantly dismiss request stating personal reasons. Jona is excited and looking forward to high school. He meets many new friends, most of them older than himself. He becomes impressed with some of the football team's players. Bobby "Bee Bee" Brown the Quarterback for the Bruisers becomes Jona's fond friend. He looks up to Bee Bee. Jona, Cuz and RJ attend all of the home games, even Blanket. The regional school district is quite large, many of the students are bussed to school; neighborhoods are extremely diverse. Bee Bee is brown skinned, average looking, very short hair, a pleasant smile, muscular athletic build.

He's from an impoverished background, he's attending the school because of an athletic award. He is the only child from a one-parent family, his mother, his father abandoned them when he was a small child. He is arguably considered the #1 quarterback in the state. Due to school, budget constraints the State Championship has been post phoned until the second week of the fall semester.

"Game night", there is no sign of Bee Bee. Questioning his mother, she stated, "He left before me as usual, what's the matter?" "He didn't show up for the game," a detective stated. Investigation reveals his mother may have been the last person to see him. Impatient for the game to start a chant begins from both sides of the stadium, loudly. "BEE BEE, WHERE ARE YOU, WHERE ARE YOU BEE BEE?" Over and over again the chant continues, for concern not as ridicule. Through concern, the game is delayed at the discretion of the coaches and officials.

A fan arriving late for the game who knows Bee Bee discovers a familiar signature type bandanna belonging to Bee Bee not far from the rear stadium entrance. Learning what is happening she turns it over to the stadium security. This causes extreme alarm.

To Jona, Cuz and R.J. their thoughts are, "something is wrong." Long before, the stadium security has informed the police, they respond.

Previously Jona on a couple of occasions had invited Bee Bee to Cuz's house to fish, play video games and go boating. Jona was impressed being the friend of a star football player. Cuz, R.J. and Blanket had taken a special liking to Bee Bee. His mannerly attitude, humility and quite speech were soothing to them.

This time there is no request. Cuz and Jona approach the police and ask if they could be of any assistance. Knowing of their reputation, the police are immediately receptive. Jona has a personal interest, he requested Bee Bee's bandanna.

Blanket being around Bee Bee before gets a very strong scent. He quickly runs in small circles barking as if to say, "Follow me." He leads them to a corner of a small somewhat secluded asphalt parking lot not too far from the rear stadium entrance. On the grassy area just off the lot, they find dug into the grass deep rounded indications of the back of shoe heels.

Sound inductive reasoning leads them to believe someone or persons didn't want Bee Bee to play in the game.

The search for Bee Bee takes priority over all else. This is at least a possible motive for his disappearance. Now it becomes a process of elimination. No one rooting for the "Bruisers" would want their star quarterback not to play in a game of this magnitude. Suspicions turn to the opposing team, some fans, coaches, gamblers, etc. Suspicions become focused but varied, anyone could be suspect, and speculation becomes puzzling.

A public announcement is made about Bee Bee's disappearance and the circumstances surrounding it. The crowd is informed the incident may possibly be an abduction; anyone having any knowledge should report it to the authorities. Now great concern sets in, the stadium is evacuated. Some students and fans retreat to a popular tavern, "Bottom's Up." Bee Bee is the topic of conversation. One particular student, Denny a fan of the opposing team, the "Falcons" becomes somewhat tipsy. Sitting at a table with several friends his slurred whispering talk becomes louder than he realizes.

"I know what happened to Bee Bee and why" he asserts. Several patrons seated at the next table overhear bits and pieces of the conversation, not knowing whether it's true or not they go to the authorities. After an interview, they don't know Denny but give a description. This may be the most crucial lead in the investigation. They immediately respond to the tavern, Denny is known there but has left with some friends, the tavern owner informs them he stays at the Si Lo Fi fraternity house on Locust Street.

Arriving at the Frat House they find Denny in somewhat of a stupor, still tipsy. They take him to the Police Station, not to be interviewed but interrogated. Jona is too young to be present but waits anxiously for the results.

"THE INTERROGATION"

Mr. Detective: "Denny do you know why you are here?"

"No sir."

"Do you know a football player named Bee Bee?"

"No, I've heard, know of him, I don't know, I've seen him before."

"Denny, we believe you're in serious trouble."

"I ain't done nothin'."

"Denny, running your mouth has gotten you in a mess; people have told us about your babbling at the tavern, you said." "I know what happened to Bee Bee and why!"

Mr. Detective: Slamming his hand against the wall, "Denny, you're about to be charged with obstruction of justice if you don't tell s everything you know right now."

Denny, Shaken and crying ask, "Am I going to jail?"

"No, to prison if you don't cooperate."

"Can I call my parents?"

"Here's the phone, call'em."

Denny calls and tells his parents that he's in jail, they respond. Mr. Detective informs them of the situation, that he needs Denny's cooperation. Denny's parents angered shaken and upset command him to cooperate with the police. Denny agrees.

"DENNY'S STORY"

"I overheard them talking." "Who is them?" Mr. Detective asks. Denny, "Randy Bryant, Doug Brown and Jay, I don't know his last name, he goes by "J.J." They were talking, planning to grab Bee Bee, hide him until the game was over and let him go. "Where were they going to hide him?" "Uh, um, I don't remember, some uh, I think some empty old building, a warehouse, a vacant camper, trailer someplace." The detectives are thinking, "Where could this be?" They inform Denny's parents he will remain in custody until he sobers up and hopefully remembers more. The three suspects are taken into custody and interrogated, they become "hard core" denying any knowledge of Bee Bee's disappearance.

The authorities and search team are befuddled as to where the area is to which Bee Bee may have been taken. Everyone is searching their individual thoughts. They have their (Thinking Caps) on. Suddenly, Mr. Detective slams his hand against the wall stating, "I know, I think I know, it must be, it must be the old vacant brewery, it's about a mile from town." "What?" Detective Josh inserts. Mr. Detective states, "The abandoned Brewery, there's junk cars, campers, trailers there, it's an eye sore."

It's beginning to become day light, the grass is covered with due, perfect for tracking. Mr. Detective states, "Jona, Cuz, this is a job for Blanket, lets search the area." With hope, prayers and fingers crossed they proceed to the Old Brewery.

Arriving, Blanket is again given the scent of Bee Bee's bandanna. First, they search the abandoned brewery, no success. Jona again gives the bandanna to Blanket for a fresh scent. Blanket roams the area, energetic and excited he knows his job, he approaches a particular abandoned trailer, there is a short 2" by 4" plank angled against the door. Jona hollers loudly with excitement, "There's something there, there's something there." Removing the wooden plank forcing the door they find Bee Bee. His wrists are tied to a sink plumbing pipe secured by a rope, his ankles secured to an old hot water tank. He is lying prone on the floor stretched out with duct tape covering his mouth. "Bingo," Needless to say everyone is relieved and elated. Bee Bee because of his physical condition seems to be "Okay." After a brief hospital exam, he is released. His mother is notified of his rescue and he is taken home.

The task now becomes continued interrogation of the three suspects, also to interview Bee Bee to get his account of just what happened. Due to the magnitude of the seriousness of the incident, the officials declare the game a forfeit in favor of the "Bruisers."

They will play in the state championship. This decision is overturned, there is no indication any of the Falcons were involved. The game is rescheduled.

Bee Bee recalls approaching the rear entrance to the stadium, it was getting dark, I felt maybe several people approaching me from the rear, I suspected joggers. Suddenly I was grabbed, a large cloth sack or bag, maybe burlap, felt like burlap, was placed over my head and shoulders. I was struggling, I thought I would suffocate. I know there were at least three or more of them. I know I was put into a van, side door. One voice kept saying, "Don't hurt him, don't hurt him." I guess my watch was lost in the struggle, I don't have it. Cuz suggest a small volunteer's search of the path of the abduction in an attempt to hopefully find the watch. Bee Bee tells them the watch was sentimental, it was given to him at an awards banquet. There is an engraving on the back, "Shelby High School, 2010"; there are only three of them.

The three suspects have been separated since they have been in custody. An inspection reveals only two are wearing watches, neither has an engraving on the back plate.

A long shot, based on Denny's testimony the Judge agrees to issue a search warrant for each suspects Frat House room. Odds for success are slim. Any fan arriving or leaving the stadium may have found the watch. Within minutes of executing the search, the watch is found in Dough Brown's nightstand. Mr. Detective asserts loudly, "We've definitely got at least one good suspect."

Back at the station, Doug is confronted with the watch. He states, "I found it." "Found it where?" Mr. Detective asks. "In the yard at the Frat House." is Dough's reply.

Did you inquire if anyone had lost a watch, "No, I was going to?" Mr. Detective informs him that he is going to be charged with Abduction, Receiving Stolen Property and Inducing Panic. You're eighteen years old, that's prison time. "What, what can I do?" Mr. Detective states as he closes the cell door "Get an attorney." Doug is upset, shaking and crying, he's thinking, "My GOD, prison, it was only a school prank, a little bet."

Now the task becomes questioning the other suspects, it's not yet an "open and shut" case. Randy and J.J. are terrified being locked up. Jona being a "Jr. Detective" has a suggestion, take Blanket to the trailer for a new scent. Put J.J. and Randy in a line-up with several volunteers, let's see who he identifies. Everyone snickers, laughing, a dog and a line-up, we'd get laughed out of court. However, another scent may be of help in someway. Cuz, yes but if it works within ourselves we would have a more concrete investigation.

Blanket is released inside the trailer, sniffing around, he begins pushing empty discarded beer cans around the floor with his nose. Mr. Detective and Josh retrieve their dusting kits; "Bingo!" They get latent prints from each can. Back at the station, they get comparisons from all three suspects. Jona's suggestion was successful after all. Confronted with all the evidence, Denny's testimony, and Doug's confession, the suspects confess and give written statements. Doug informs the police the three of them had a large bet against the other team.

After a speedy trial they are convicted, sentenced to two years, Doug is sentenced to two and a half years due to the Receiving Stolen Property.

The "Bruisers" win the rescheduled game and go to the State Championship. Does Blanket understand? He knows from praises, petting and a special dinner he has done a Great Job.

"BLANKET GETS DOGNAPPED"

Jona and Blanket take the small outboard motor boat across the lake to the Marina to buy fishing tackle and sundries. Jona docks the boat and goes into the store. Blanket as many times before jumps onto the dock to wait; he enjoys watching the people and the boats docking and leaving. Jona completing his shopping returns to the boat, no Blanket! Jona becomes unraveled, throws the bags in the boat calling and whistling for Blanket, no response. He runs back in the store yelling at the clerk, "Give me the phone, give me the phone." He calls Cuz who informs him he's on his way.

Arriving, Jona and Cuz cruise the area. Cuz keeps telling Jona, "We'll find him. We'll find him." Cuz calls Mr. Detective on his cell phone frantically informing him that Blanket is missing. "Meet me at the house." "On my way," Mr. Detective replies. At the house, R.J. is attempting to console Jona without success. Everyone is pacing, walking in circles and trying to think! "Reward" Cuz screams out loud, "Reward, Blanket is a famous dog, someone snatched him." "Right." Mr. Detective retorts. By now Josh has arrived, he wants a picture of Blanket to take to Kinko's to have reward posters made. "Ten thousand dollars" Cuz says off the top of his head. Mr. Detective, "We need to settle down, we don't even have a plan, we don't know where to start." Cuz states, "The Marina, put posters at the Marina first, someone had to see something." Day has turned into night then morning.

Mr. Detective calls a friend Rollie at the FBI for help, from past experience, they know Blanket but it is out of their jurisdiction, they wish they could help. Jona is solemnly withdrawn, never ending tears states, "I'll kill him, bite him Blanket, bite him, and run away."

Later during the day several different boaters and fishermen seeing the poster report they recall two male Whites carrying a dog from the Marina, he was biting, scratching and yelping. The one had the dog in sort of a bear hug, trying to muzzle his mouth with his hand. Their descriptions didn't vary much. They were carrying fishing poles and a tackle box walking real fast to the parking lot and looking back. The witnesses gave minute descriptions.

One had a scraggly brownish beard, the other was clean-shaven. Both had on ball caps, one had Hornets written on it, gray or light blue, the other had long dark hair, and both wore sunglasses, they were wearing jeans, one had those shredded ragged parts on the knees.

Sympathy, help and prayer calls are constantly coming in on the phone from well-wishers. One caller states, "We've got your dog Blanket, twenty thousand, you'll get him back alive." (Hang-up)

The call is bittersweet, hopefully Blanket is alive, at least they have some substance as to what happened and why. Mr. Detective thinks, "Ransom, ransom, ransom, that's the key word, now the FBI can get involved." After another call, he is told they need a second call. Everyone is now anxiously awaiting and hoping for a second call. Finally, it comes, "No police, twenty thousand." (Hang–up) Cuz's phone list "Unavailable Caller."

"Okay, that's it, I'll call my friend back at the FBI," Mr. Detective says picking up the phone. "Hey Rollie, we got the second call, now what?" Hesitation, "Call you back, hour or two, Okay."

Minutes seem like hours waiting on the return call, finally it comes. "This is Rollie, give me Will." Will takes the phone. "Okay, we've got the go ahead, listen carefully, about three hours' drive; myself and two other agents Smith & Wilson, casual dress. You know me, we'll meet you at your closest inconspicuous diner, dress casual. I need the name of an inconspicuous diner." "Uh, uh, Brown Rooster, route 18 at Cross road." "Okay, about three hours, only you and Cuz, again dress causal."

During the meeting, the agents are briefed on the situation, description, witnesses, etc.

"THE PLAN"

Agent Rollie explains in detail how the operation is to proceed:

1. Cuz cannot leave the house, he's the only one that answers the phone.

2. Need a recent photograph of Blanket.

3. No visitors.

4. We will move our monitoring equipment in after dark and remove our vehicle.

5. Will, disguised with a long beard, sunglasses and coveralls pretending to do yard work only at the front of the house, otherwise take care of your normal duties. These guys are familiar with you, they'll probably be watching the house. We'll cover the rear.

6. Any car parked or out of the ordinary or slowly driving by get the plate number and type vehicle if possible. Once instructions come if any, we'll have to draw up a plan of action immediately, like yesterday.

Agent Rollie, "Everyone understands." They answer in the affirmative. "Okay, let's get started. Everyone will have a small two-way radio for constant communication, restricted channel. Agent Wilson will casually be surveying the area by car."

Everything is in place. It's now an antagonizing, hurry up and wait game. Another phone call stating, "Are you ready for the exchange?" Cuz relates to the caller he wants a photograph of Blanket with a piece of blue material around his neck. "Okay, Okay, You're not in a position to play games with me, we don't play games." Cuz, "I'm waiting for the photograph," then hangs up as instructed. Agent Rollie. "I believe they're in a frenzy now, scared, shook up and confused, no plan as of yet."

Jona is somewhat calmed down, semi optimistic but still rattled, eyes red from tears & rubbing.

The picture arrives. "Right guys" says Rollie. "Now we'll get another call stating their plans for the exchange, no doubt they've had the house under surveillance." Agent Rollie, "I don't believe these guys have a plan, just opportunity on spur of the moment. Blanket is a popular dog."

Non-Residents have to be checked in at the security gate. Only a resident can have a visitor's name put on the pass list with a temporary windshield sticker at the security gate. Cuz suggest they contact security for help. Rollie states, "Good idea Cuz, however, too many people having information of our investigation could innocently jeopardize it." Cuz understands. Agent Wilson reports on two occasions he observed an old brown Chevy pick-up that passed the house twice two days in a row, slow speed, muddy bent up plates (in State), numbers one & eight, letters V & R, the rest were unreadable. It has a metal canopy over the bed and a trailer hitch.

After receiving the information, Agent Rollie informs everyone not to get too excited but we may have two suspects. He couldn't get close enough to get a facial or clothing description. Again, it's hurry up and wait.

Another phone call. "Hello Cuz, know who this is?" "No." Cuz nervously replies, "What now!"

"Go to the Stop Shop near the lake entrance, tell them your phone is out of order and you're expecting an important call. Wear a ball cap with the bill turned to the right, fifteen minutes." (Hang-up)

Cuz following orders complies. Another call comes in, caller, "Go to the Sport Shop at the Marina right now, purchase a red and black back pack, there's only one left, no tricks, return home." Again, Cuz complies.

Returning home Cuz gives the small tape recorder, Agent Rollie had given him. The agents listen.

"First timers, Agent Wilson retorts, "Punks trying to be a pro, that's in our favor." Meanwhile a photo of Blanket arrives with the blue scarf around his neck.

The task becomes nerve racking to everyone except the agents. The agents inform Cuz they would like to make a quick arrest, however, if it takes longer, private bedrooms, video games, exercise room and food! Agent Smith jokingly states, "Wish I could move in here without my wife." Wilson, "That goes for me also." (Laughter) "Be my guest." Cuz states with a grin.

Smiling, Agent Rollie, due to his experience asserts, "Get serious, next call will probably be it, we'll have to think fast, have a counter plan at moment's notice." Phone rings, Cuz answers, a different caller this time, in a fake Amish voice states.

"Okay, you got' a money and uh backpack, call'ah you in the morning with instructions for the exchange." "Wait", Cuz says. (Hang-up) Agent Wilson, "Probably a cell, can't trace it until we have it."

Agent Rollie calls Mr. Detective. "Here we go man, you'll need a pick-up truck with several bales of straw in the bed, park it in the driveway tonight, same disguise, you'll spend the night. We're waiting for more instructions." Everyone is standing by waiting for the phone to ring. The decision is that Jona is too young to be put in Harm's Way. Cuz only has his cell, he may be searched.

Next morning before daybreak Agent Rollie has Will spot the bales of straw around the front yard. Wilson is standing by not far from the security gate. Wilson is patrolling the area. Jona, Cuz and R.J. waiting are near crazy, pins and needles. Blanket can't help them this time. Phone rings, "Hey Cuz listens," a bark and yelp is heard, no proof its Blanket. "Eleven AM, be ready to drive." (Hang-up)

Exactly eleven AM phone rings, same question. "Hey Cuz you ready?" "Yeah." "You got the backpack filled with the money!" "Yeah." "Drive out the front gate to Highway #32 east bound, all instructions from now on will be on your cell phone, hope it's charged, (laughter) joke Cuz." Cuz following instructions, ring, ring. "Yeah," Cuz answering. Voice, "If I ever call and your phone is busy, it's Blanket's problem." (Hang-up)

Driving east on the highway Cuz is wondering, "Where the hell am I going?" Everyone is surveilling Cuz at a safe and secure distance.

Cell phone, ring, ring, "Yes, what now" answers Cuz. "You're going to the "Old Indian Serpent Burial Grounds," the tourist attraction, forty minutes, arriving, park in the visitor's parking lot and wait." Cuz is sweating, apprehensive and scared to death, he's thinking, please, please, please get this over with.

Agent Rollie, "Where are you guys? Damn, this is the blind leading the blind." "We've got him, Old Serpent Burial Grounds, the tourist attraction." "I'm on 32 East; Wilson is on 32 West, each of us is about 100 to 150 yards away from the entrance, Okay!" Rollie, "Just don't have any intersecting trails or roads between you and the visitor's entrance, I'm on my way, Okay." "Covered boss." (Ditto)

Agent Rollie enters the visitor's area carrying a small picnic cooler, all frequency radio," Six Pack," battery generated "Boom Box," stack of paper cups and plates: he displays on a picnic table as though he is waiting for some friends to arrive.

He contacts everyone, lets them know he's in place waiting for Cuz to show, he knows he's somewhere on the grounds. Cuz appears, he's been told to go the overhead picnic shelter, find an empty table, sit on the bench and place the backpack at his feet. Someone with a cane will approach the table, when he's about thirty yards away, get up leave the backpack; drive your car down the entrance road, pull to the side just before reaching the highway, someone will meet you. Suspect #2 calls suspect #1 stating, "A piece of cake, the backpack has turned green with paper," Okay, return the merchandise, pick me up in front of the tourist station.

Cuz complies with his orders. Suddenly the gray dented truck described as suspicious earlier pulls off the side of the road behind Cuz. A male White, long beard dressed in Amish attire approaches Cuz. In fake Amish brogue he states, "You lik'a dogs." "Special dogs." "Yeah, I got'a one, you can'a have it, wait." He raises the canopy on the truck bed, retrieves Blanket who is muzzled and scraping, throws him in the window of Cuz's car and states, "Take ah off." He gets in his truck, makes a U-Turn and picks up his partner. Nothing unusual they assume all is well, a feeling of confidence.

Joyful and happy they drive west on Highway 32. Rollie alerts all units not to stop the truck until it pulls over someplace. Agent Smith, the comedian states, "Dumb asses, Amish man driving a truck, guess he left his horse and buggy at that Marathon station back the road for a tune-up and wheel alignment." Agent Rollie covering his mouth trying not to laugh retorts, "Knock it off Smitty, we're still in the middle of serious business, everyone got everyone covered." "Yes sir" (Ditto): "Their first stop we're taking them, I want them vulnerable, pants down and exposed out of the truck, OK!" "Yes sir." (Dittos)

The suspects driving on the highway begin to chat. #2: Taking off his Amish clothes and fake beard, pitching them to the side of the road states, "Man, we rich, we did it. Let's stop and get a bite to eat I'm starving. No fast food stuff, one of those Out Back or Red Lobsters, no beer, real drinks." Suspect #1 I forms #2, "First stop we'll put the money in the empty tool box in the truck bed. Get rid of the backpack. We have to be safe, plan ahead." "Yeah man, it's your game stay ahead of it." "Hell we need gas, anything we buy we'll use our own money." "Okay, you got it." "Oh there's a Shell station just ahead, I got to raise the river."

I'll meet you back at the truck." Suspect #2: Exiting the rest room, backpack discarded in the trash can. Agents' guns drawn, "Hands-Up, right now." Suspect #2 obeys the command, no resistance. Suspect #1 after paying for the gas walking back to the truck, "Under arrest" in a loud voice states Agent Smith and Wilson, suspect #1 begins to run, he's chased and tackled by Agent Wilson. The backpack is retrieved from the rest room trash container. Every tenth bill in the money packets has been marked.

Cuz still driving home afraid to make a phone call, stops removes Blanket's muzzle, Blanket is relieved. Cuz not aware of what has taken place arrives home. The reunion is unbelievable and cannot be described. Rollie contacts Cuz and informs him of their success, not to worry, these guys are going away for almost ever, see you shortly.

Just to lend credence to the case, in court, Blanket would be of significant importance. In an (In-Camera) hearing three Judges all players and suspects are present. Blanket is given a scent from the discarded Amish attire discarded off the roadside, he then attacks Suspect #2. After a thorough search of the vehicle, the money is recovered from the toolbox. Before a Jury, there is a finding of guilty. The sentence is to be ten years with no probability of parole.

Suspect #1 is Timothy Ford, warrant for Child Support, capiases, numerous traffic warrants, and assault.

Suspect #2 is Trace Gordon, no previous record.

The residents at the lake had no knowledge of the incident. One of the home owners at Lake Shore was on a bowling team with Tim Ford and offered him a visitor's pass to the lake on a couple of occasions to fish from the public dock. Hearing about Blanket, He constructed the dog napping.

Finally, a full day of celebration for all, even Miss Fran who has yet to be told another rescue story. Jona and Blanket have fully recovered from the incident. The Agents and families have been invited.

PART TWO

(Four Years Later)

"GRADUATION/REUNION"

"Cap and Gown," its Jona's high school graduation. At the last word of the commencement speech, Caps and Tassels block out the beautiful blue sky. Screams, whistling and roars drown out every other sound. Finally, there are soft voices, mouth to ear whispers and caresses. The reality of one of life's first meaningful accomplishments. Cuz, R.J., Mr. Detective, Miss Fran, friends, some rescued, seems everyone is there. R.J. as always has planned the "After Party." Diploma in hand, grinning from ear-to-ear he approaches Cuz, hands him his diploma, with a smiling face states, "Here this is yours." Cuz holding back his emotions hugs Jona caressing the diploma against his bosom. Blanket can't be there but he'll share this moment with him later in some special way.

Cuz, "Oh, by the way Jona some big, I mean big Black guy wants to see you. "Why, for what?" Jona ask, Cuz, "I don't know, that's him with his back to us talking to your Head Master." "I ain't going over there, I haven't done anything." "You can't hide. I guarantee he'll find you."

Jona approaches the rear of the Big Black guy talking to the Head Master, as the Master leans forward he says, "Hi Jona, congratulations." The Big Black guy turns, grabs Jona under his arms and lifts him above his head stating, "Hey Li'l Bro couldn't miss this, my Guardian Angel." "BEE, BEE." is Jona's overwhelming response. "God you've grown, you're a giant." "Meet my family, Thelma my wife and three, year old Tony. Tony this is your uncle Jona." Taken back Jona with the heels of his hands is wiping back tears. "Uncle, you mean Uncle."

"Sure you're family." Jona, "He's cute, Miss Thelma you're beautiful." Thank you Jona and you're very handsome. Bee Bee, "How's my one and only dog?" "Great." The four of them excusing themselves to hook-up with Cuz and RJ.

"Cuz, I'm an uncle." "Congratulations." "Jona, walk us to the car, Cuz will fill you in later. I have so many commitments and responsibilities, it's overwhelming. Hate to miss your party, but I promise I'll make it up to you."

Bee, Bee opens the trunk, pulls out an autographed San Diego football jersey (To Jona from Bee, Bee) "I'm a second year wide receiver with the San Diego Chargers, that's me, number "84", you'll hear from me in a week or two." Jona is stunned, almost speechless, "Bee, Bee this is real." "Guess so, love you Li'l Bro, and take care, give Blanket a pat, where's my hug Li'l Bro." They caress, "Bye."

Arriving home for the After Party the cap and gown disappear. The number #84 jersey swallowing Jona is boastfully displayed, autograph and all. As usual, R.J. has left no stone unturned. Miss Fran who attended the graduation has baked several cakes and a special lemon pie. Everyone has and unforgettable time. Afterwards Cuz informs Jona that he'll get his graduation gift later. Jona responds, "I've got everything, I don't need another gift."

Next morning as the sun comes up over Jona's favorite distant hilly range, blinding his eyes he realizes he over indulged in the day before's long activity. Turning his face away from the sun, Blanket pulling at the cover, he awakes rubbing his eyes. Looking down he realizes he fell asleep in his jersey, which he will wear all day.

Coming home from College every other weekend, he and Blanket have become adjusted. Now he has something else to become adjusted to.

After breakfast Jona humbly states, "I want to have a talk." R.J. "Here it comes Cuz, bring it on Jona, I've been waiting for this." "For what?" "What's she look like? I know she's pretty." "Well wait a minute R.J. you're going to fast." "Hope you aren't, bring it on." Cuz says, "I like this little talk already, you're not little Jona anymore." "You guys are confusing me, making this difficult." Cuz, "Jona this is not a rescue, (laughing) maybe it is, yours or hers, invite her parents over for a picnic and boating, that's easy." R.J. "First of all, does she have a name?" "Brooke." "Unique, I like that." "She only lives an hour from here." "Okay, sure set it up!" "R.J., how did you know?" "Women know about the Birds and the Bees, men know about the Rabbits and the Squirrels, I'm sure Cuz will give you a lesson, he's an expert. By the way your driver license test is 11AM tomorrow."

Jona on the phone to Brooke, "See if Saturday or Sunday is OK for lunch and boating, bring swim wear, call me as soon as you know." Brooke calls back, "Saturday is fine, 10AM Okay?' "Sure." The driver test is flying colors. Jona and Brooke are on pins and needles waiting for Saturday. Finally, it arrives. R.J. doesn't want to over-do anything, steaks, hamburgers, metts, potato salad, fruit salad and baked beans, simple.

Saturday, a beautiful day. A very comfortable introduction by everyone. Kevin, Brooke's father is medium height, graying hair, neatly combed, handsome, Blanch, her mother, is attractive, short-cropped hair, rosy cheeks average build.

Brooke, somewhat a stunner, shoulder length hair, rosy cheeks like her mother, personality plus. Jona, "And this is Blanket, say hello," Blanket responds with a bark. A quick tour of the house and grounds. Tea and juice with a short brunch under the canopy on the dock getting acquainted, small talk. Jona and Brooke are absorbed in the game room.

After confirming Brooke can swim, with life jackets they take a ride in the outboard, with Blanket at the bow, his favorite spot. Needless to say, Brooke and her parents are impressed. This has never been Cuz or R.J.'s intention, just to make guest just comfortable, but also to truly enjoy themselves.

Question and answer games begin with the two ladies. "How did you guys meet?" "In the library, studying." "The library!" "What do you do when you're not studying?" "Take a walk, go to a movie." Cuz, "Kevin, the crappie are running, I've got poles on the dock, want to catch a few." "Sure, I believe this is our exit." "What else do you kids do when you're not in the library studying?" Jona grabs Brooke by the hand he retorts, "Excuse us, come on Brooke," they walk to and enter the house, returning in a few minutes.

The ladies, questionably frowning at each other puzzled. Jona, "I just kissed Brooke for the first time, any other questions?" R.J. and Blanch, embarrassed realize they have gone outside the limits. R.J. "Well, let's go boating." Blanch is impressed with Jona's straightforward honesty; RJ is not surprised. A tour of the lake like Cuz has taken guest on before is extremely peaceful and pleasant.

Getting more acquainted there are questions about college life from the parents. Kevin reveals he is a computer analyst for Toyota, Blanch a homemaker as R.J., something in common. Cuz states he is a small time investor. Everyone returns to the dock for a great lunch. Cuz tells Jona to invite Miss Fran, "Great idea, be right back." After lunch, Jona and Brooke leave the adults and disappear to the house. Jona shows Brooke his scrapbook, which he and R.J. have complied. Brooke is amazed, "You never mentioned any of this to me." "Well it would seem like bragging."

Meanwhile Miss Fran is reporting some of the rescue stories to Kevin and Blanch as though she was there, very enjoyable, exciting to listen to. Kevin and Blanch tell everyone what a fine visit it was and expect to return the favor more than once. In private before leaving Brooke tells Jona what a great kiss it was, "We need to engage in that activity more often."

During the drive home, everyone is talking at the same time. "By the way Kevin, your daughter just had her first kiss." "Mom, that wasn't my first kiss, it was my first by Jona, it was the best kiss." All those rescues, Cuz never mentioned any of them until Miss Fran came over, he's a very easy man to like, humble. "Yeah, so is Jona, handsome huh Mom." "Yes dear." "Dad, do you know a Bee Bee Brown, plays football with the San Diego Chargers, he came to the graduation because of Jona, their family like, made Jona his son's uncle. "He's one hell of a player!" Everyone agrees they've had quite a day.

"SPECIAL INVITE"

-The Phone Call-

"Cuz, it's Bee Bee, I need to run something by you before talking to Li'l Bro." "Okay what is it?"

"Our pre-season game is two weeks out. I want to make all the arrangements at my expense. You'll have game passes, even to the locker room, ladies excluded. Thelma will hook up with R.J. show her around the town, the sights, shopping, whatever. You and Jona will meet some of my teammates, autographs, pictures and all. I'll give you dates tomorrow, hope you're available, talk it over, this is my private number. By the way I have more than enough room."

"Okay, got it." Cuz hangs up, says to himself, "Hell yes we'll be there, hell yes." Cuz informs Jona and R.J. of the invitation, Jona's response is "Are you shitting me, are you shitting me?" Cuz surprised by Jona's language, laughing displays a response of excitement, happiness even disbelief himself, again, loudly, "Hell yes, we'll be there, take that to the bank."

Both Jona and Cuz individually in their own minds are apprehensively fantasizing the coming weekend. They visualize Bee Bee running at least three or four touchdowns, no fumbles or missed catches, a perfect game. Wow, serious thought, "What if Bee Bee gets injured," the thought is immediately dismissed. Jona and Cuz are average football fans but now more than ever they begin to enhance their knowledge of the game. They buy "Sports Illustrated," ESPN, read the sports section of the newspaper every day and watch the sport channels. The apprehension and suspense grows what clothes should they take, what will they wear game day, should they buy new sneakers?" Jona knows he will wear his special number 84 football jersey. R.J. realizes this has become a very serious task. Decisions are made and changed daily. Both are bedazzled.

They start playing "one on one" football in the yard. R.J. watching from the rear window enjoys their clumsy antics, neither are athletic.

Now here comes Jona with another humble head down "We need to talk, syndrome." R.J. says "Bring it on Jona, the birds and the bees, squirrels, rabbits are past history, now what?" "Well, well Bee Bee said I could bring a friend." "Here it comes Cuz, Brooke is the friend." "You think you know everything R.J.," with a humble grin. "I'm a woman." Cuz tells Jona it would be Okay with them, however the final decision is up to Brooke's parents, Kevin and Blanch. Cuz, to Jona, "Brooke is to know nothing about this conversation, understood!" Jona, "Yes sir." Cuz and R.J. discuss the matter in private. R.J. believes it would be the start of a bonding between her and Brooke, what ever that may lead to.

Cuz its Bee Bee, "What's it look like?" "Everything is an anxious, GO, one question!" "Okay".

"Jona wants to know if his friend, girlfriend, sort of, Go-a-long with R.J. and Thelma. "No problem here, Okay. We have a room for everyone, bring your putter, I've got my own putting green, tennis court, pool, video room, exercise room, the works. You've got a six-hour drive, see you early Friday morning; you won't understand after the game Sunday, I'll be in pain, comes with the profession, the consequences, the real world of football, I might be able to say, thanks for coming, That's it, see you early Friday morning, bye." R.J. is charged with the duty of contacting Brooke's parents about the weekend invitation.

"Hello Blanch, it's R.J., how you doing?" "We're fine, how bout ya'll." "Okay, I'm a bit uncomfortable, I need to ask you something!" R.J. explains the weekend invitation in detail requesting Brooke come along. "It's mostly a girly thing with Thelma, Bee Bee's wife and myself. The men's thing is football, football and more football." Blanch, "Sounds great to me, I'll pass it along to Kevin, call you back, by the way I'm sending you a note regarding the wonderful hospitality." "That's not necessary, we enjoyed the visit."

Kevin and Blanch are upper middle class, both well educated. Their only concern is Brooke's college education regarding tuition. Kevin is delighted about the invitation, he approves without hesitation. Blanch calls R.J. and informs her they are very receptive to the invitation and feel good about the offer. R.J. is relieved, all is taken care of, she informs Jona. He is delighted at the news, calls Brooke right away. Cuz has talked to Miss Fran, she is excited to "Doggy Sit" Blanket, they get along well.

The drive to San Diego is dominated with football conversation between Jona and Cuz. R.J. and Brooke make themselves oblivious to the front seat conversation, they have soft girly conversation of their own. Upon arrival, Thelma makes everyone, family comfortable. She informs them Bee Bee is at morning practice, shows them to their rooms the house and grounds, everyone is impressed. Thelma introduces everyone to Bee Bee's mother, Mama, who lives with them. "Where's Tony?" Jona ask, "At the nursery until later." Bee Bee will be home soon for a short break, he has plans for the guys. We need to make plans for us ladies, sightseeing, lunch and especially shopping, R.J. "By the way Brooke," she hands Brooke an envelope. This is your graduation present from

Cuz to go shopping." Brooke, holding back tears. "Don't do this please." "If you want a fight see Cuz, us girls are going shopping." Brooke excuses herself goes to her room, opens the envelope containing more than a modest amount of money. After wiping her tears, she returns.

Mama tells Jona how pretty Brooke is, head down he blushes. "I know." Mama, always in the kitchen, heavy set, graying hair, glasses down over the tip of her nose, always at least one hand on her hip and never without an apron. Mama lives with Bee Bee, Thelma and Tony.

Jona and Cuz are browsing and fascinated by Bee Bee's trophy room. Trophy upon trophy from high school, junior college to the draft. Pictures, even one with the President San Diego Fan and several teammates. Jona and Cuz read and study everything. Mama announces, "Foods Ready", always-southern breakfast every morning and soul food rest of the day "Got a keep that big boy fed."

Jona and Brooke try to play tennis, then some fun on the putting green before returning to the game room. Cuz is still reading and re reading every article and magazine in the trophy room. R.J. and Thelma close in age seem to develop an instant rapport, they definitely let Brooke realize she is one of the trio. Mama likes telling funny stories along with her own jokes, which make everyone, giggle and laugh. She doesn't share with them the struggles she and Bee Bee have endured, her teen pregnancy; Bee Bee's father disappearing shortly after Bee Bee was born, single mother all her life. She is a strong woman who has learned somehow, let the past be the past. Her pride and love is Bee Bee, her Joy is Tony and Thelma, and her prayers have always been "GOD."

Bee Bee arrives for a light lunch greets everyone and meets Brooke. "Gosh Li'l Bro, you can sure pick'em." He gets a snap kiss from Thelma, Tony and Mama. "Guys we're off, noon work outs!" Conversation on the way to the practice field is more about reminiscing Bee Bee's rescue than football. Bee Bee, "Jona you got a camera, if not I got one in my locker." "I got it, wouldn't leave it for anything."

Entering the locker room and being introduced Jona and Cuz are amazed at the reception they get. The disproportionate sizes of the players, sort of small to huge giants. The players make Jona and Cuz feel very comfortable, telling team's jokes about Bee Bee and having laughs. Taking pictures and signing autographs. Jona is presented with an official autographed football with most of the players' names. Totally unexpected and surprised Jona and Cuz are stunned speechless.

The players hit the field, Jona and Cuz are in the stands taking picture after picture, and even the Coach takes a picture with both of them letting them know the entire team knows of their rescue efforts, especially Bee Bee's. Jona and Cuz are overwhelmingly, overwhelmed! "This is real, this is us Jona, me and you, beyond my imagination."

Jona can't refuse rotating the autographed football looking at the signatures and holding it against his chest, arms folded as if he were running for a touchdown. They are awed by the strenuous practice, work out drills and numerous plays they run. While the team has a short strategy meeting, Jona and Cuz wait at the car discussing the events of the day.

The drive home Jona can't shut up. Bee Bee says, "Jona you're making my ears hurt." "I can't wait to show the pictures and football to everyone, Bee Bee, this is one of the most special days of my life." "That makes me feel great Jona." Cuz "It was truly, extremely an amazing, memorable day Bee Bee, I can't describe my feelings or thankfulness."

At the house, Jona is the Master of Ceremony reliving, talking, and explaining every minute detail with the utmost enthusiasm. Everyone is "off the hook" with exciting enjoyment, as though they were there.

Even Tony is an attentive audience even though he may not understand he enjoys Jona's antics, he's beginning to pronounce Uncle Jona with some confusion. Jona is flattered being called uncle.

Time to relax on the deck, chitchat and listen to Jona all over again. Take a swim or whatever. Mama has barbequed short ribs, collard greens macaroni and cheese, candied yams, corn on the cob, cornbread, a baked carrot cake and lemon meringue pie. She learned from R.J. that was Jona's favorite. After supper, Bee Bee soaks in the hot tub relieving the pain he has endured at practice. Jona and Brooke take a swim, a walk and then movies. R.J. and Thelma give Mama a hand in the kitchen and plan for tomorrow's "Girly Day". Everyone retires early. Brooke calls her parents informing them how unbelievable the trip has been already and her graduation gift from Cuz.

The aroma from Mama's breakfast, bacon, sausage, grits with cheese, eggs and cheese, pancakes and coffee allows everyone to wake in the morning with a fruit and sweet roll tray. It makes everyone's eyes bigger than their stomach. The ladies prepare to go shopping and sight seeing. Jona becomes consumed with Tony. Cuz and Bee Bee relax with small manly talk before approaching the putting green. Bee Bee tells Cuz he doesn't play tennis. The court came with the house.

After some putting practice, the sun becoming uncomfortable Bee Bee and Cuz return to the shaded deck. A picture of iced tea for Bee Bee and a couple of early cold beers for Cuz. The ladies have departed on their journey.

Cuz, "Bee Bee, I need to enlighten you about Jona, Okay." "Yeah, Okay Cuz." He relays every detail of he and Jona's life, survival in the snowy blizzard with Blanket and a small brown bear, Jona calls Three Legs. Having flashbacks of his parents' tragic deaths along with his aunt and uncle. My self not knowing Jona existed until he was twelve years old, biological cousins.

Bee Bee with hands clasped on his lap, his chin against his chest, turning his head from side to side. The story deeply penetrating his emotions, it bites his soul. "Cuz, I am as I know you are so thankful and proud the Lord and fate brought him to us, brought him to so many." "Bee Bee Jona never talks about any of the tragic experiences he has endured in his life or rescue ventures." "I'll never mention it to anyone except Thelma, come on I'll show you some game tapes, it'll rest our minds." Meanwhile the ladies are getting very well acquainted, R.J. and Thelma are comfortable age wise, and Brooke the younger fits in well, her personality, humor and intelligence. She's not a kid, rather a young lady. They openly tell stories about themselves, the first time they got tipsy, their mischief in college, first boyfriend and so on.

They observe the naval ships, beautiful scenic parks, drive to El Capistrano where the Swallows return the same day every year. They have a wonderful outside lunch on the dock over the water. Thelma tells them about the history of San Diego. They attend Thelma's favorite inexpensive shopping area. Brooke buys souvenirs and gifts for her parents. Worn out they return home and share most of their day.

After a brief nap, everyone smells Mama's menu. Roast turkey and dressing, mashed potatoes with gravy, green bean casserole, left over collards and short ribs, homemade yeast rolls and dessert.

Jona remarks, "Dag, it's not Thanksgiving." "Got to keep that Big Boy fed." Mama replies.

After supper, Jona and Brooke play football with Tony before his bedtime. During Bee Bee's brief absence Thelma quickly explains: Bee Bee will go into the trophy room alone, review some films, have a brief social time, excuse himself, sleep in one of the guest rooms with a football in his arms psyching up for the game, remembering plays, whatever! "Up at 5:30 AM, a peanut butter and jelly sandwich or grits and molasses. That's what he was raised on, and all Mama could afford, superstition I guess! That's what got him here, guess he thinks that's what'll keep him here." Mama asserts. Mama hasn't been to a game since high school, doesn't want to see her baby get hurt, watches the tapes after each game.

During the drive to the stadium hardly a word is spoken the tension grows. Seated on the fifty, yard line as the players are announced anxiety turns to excitement. Bee Bee has his personal rooting section. "Kick-Off," every one is tense throughout the close game. The Chargers lose 21-24 in the last minutes. Jona and Cuz feel great, Bee Bee had one touchdown and eighty, three yards in receptions, no fumbles.

Bee Bee shows dejection about the loss, suffering the physical soreness, aches and pains that are part of the game, yet he feels great about his game performance. After a brief, sort of "in the huddle" recap. Bee Bee and Thelma excuse themselves, a soak in the tub and massage for Bee Bee. After returning, Mama's menu: Chicken and dumplings, green beans, stewed tomatoes, biscuits and desert. Bee Bee informs everyone he is retiring for the night wishing a safe trip. He informs them he'll call in a couple of days. Everyone tells him and Thelma what a special weekend it was, they bid farewell with hugs and kisses.

The trip home everyone is reminiscing and talking at the same time. They drop Brooke off who can't wait to tell her parents of magnificent weekend. Jona retrieves Blanket, they rejoice, everyone settles in!

"THE GIFT"

Jona and Blanket are on the dock fishing, R.J. calls Jona, "Come on up, Cuz needs you for something." They respond. Jona, "What you want Cuz?" "Here's a short list, ride up to Stop & Shop pick these items up, here's the keys." Jona and Blanket approaching the driveway observe a small Toyota blocking the driveway. Jona, "Cuz, there's a strange car blocking our driveway." "It's not a strange car Jona, it's your graduation present." "My what? I wasn't expecting a graduation present, are you shitting me?" "I know you weren't expecting one but you deserve one, now go to the store." Jona, running, crying and screaming, running to the car, "It's mine, it's mine." Blanket running behind, not understanding is happily barking.

Jona is jumping with joy in circles, Blanket is spinning in circles imitating Jona, knowing from Jona's reaction it's something good. Jona runs back to Cuz, hugging him and then to R.J. He and Blanket run and jump into the car. Riding around the lake numerous times, Blanket's head is out the window enjoying the rush of air in his face, barking. They don't return for hours, apologizing to Cuz. He informs Jona it was a fake shopping list, he didn't need the items. Jona and Blanket sleep in the car overnight. Awakening in the morning he calls Brooke and in detail describes what has happened, she is overjoyed.

"TONY IS MISSING"

Cuz answers the ringing phone! In a frantic emotional voice, Bee Bee shouts," Cuz, its Bee Bee." "What's wrong Bee Bee?" "Somebody stole Tony, kidnapped, abducted whatever! Can you drive down? I can't believe this, first me, now Tony, how can I live with this?" "Drive, hell no, I'll get a plane from Marvin, be there in less than two hours." Cuz is still apprehensive about flying, however, the flight home from Paris eased some of his fear. "Okay Cuz thanks." Cuz calls Marvin's Air-Land Transportation Service, Inc. He informs Marvin who has Certified Pilot License among other credentials to meet him at the airport as soon as possible. "OK Cuz, done, like yesterday."

During the flight, Cuz informs Jona and Marvin of Bee Bee's phone call. Upon arrival, they are informed that a "Quasi Ransom" phone call has already been received stating, "We've got Tony, and you've got money!" (Hang-up) The police and FBI have already been notified, the FBI is in route. Mama is attending Thelma who is devastated, hysterical, in a state of shock: clenched fist, shivering, has to be slightly medicated by the family physician. The FBI arrives, everyone is introduced.

Agent Fox nicknamed "Foxy" male White, slightly overweight, balding, mid-fifties, a great storyteller and jokester except when on assignment as the (AIG) Agent in Charge. The other agents are Barry "Bear" Wright and Alex O'Neal somewhat less experienced but have outstanding performance records in the bureau. Foxy recalls hearing stories of Jona, Blanket and Cuz's previous adventures; he has a very receptive attitude about them offering any assistance. Clandestinely they secure their car in the garage and set up their phone monitoring system.

Bee Bee informs every one of the situation as he was told:

The pre-school attendant Tina took Bee Bee and his five group mates to the park on their scheduled hour. They walked from the play area to the pond to feed the ducks, which as I understand was routine.

Sitting on the bench Tina was watching the kids, her purse close by when a man described as a Black male walked behind the bench, grabbed her purse and took off running. She chased him screaming "Stop him, stop him." No one responded. After a very short distance, he pitched the purse. Turning back the kids excited and screaming, "Miss Tina, Miss Tina" pointing, "That man running, he's got Tony."

Tina's story is that she screamed, "Help, help call the police that man running took one of my kids," pointing in a direction of the kids. None of the bystanders saw a man running, however some people hesitantly started running in the direction indicated to no avail. The police arrived, called for assistance and began searching the park. Tina gave the police a vague description of what she described as "In a flash" a male running, his back to me, running fast but I never saw Tony. Two police officers question a young couple sitting on a bench at the edge of the park inform them they saw a young White male carrying a and dragging a small Black boy who was kicking and crying, they thought at the time it was because of the child's misbehavior, they commented to each other. "Guess he's been a <u>bad</u> boy!"

They entered the passenger's side of a light blue or grayish compact, dingy faded paint, it sped off real fast. This information is relayed to Agents Bear, Wilson, and the police.

The Agents call for more Agents to respond so they can continue monitoring the home. Agents Bear and Wilson responds to the school. O'Neal is questioning the children.

Agent Fox, "Bee Bee, tell us everything you can so we can begin our investigation. "We enrolled Tony in pre-school, "Wee Folks" several months ago. He liked it, everything was fine." Bee Bee, pacing the floor back and forth walking in circles slapping his forehead hard with the heel of his hand, tears streaming down his cheeks states. "I don't know man, I just don't know, I get this call from the school telling me somebody took my son, damn. Uh, uh, I don't know man, uh, something about uh, in the park, uh feeding the ducks, I just don't know, why Tony? I mean, just get my son back, find my son, please find my son. First me now my son." "We're going to do everything we can, we've already started."

Agents Fox and Wright respond to the school to interview the Owner/Director of the school, Mrs. Simone Wilson, an attractive delightful lady in her mid-fifties. Tony's caretaker Tina Caldwell, a twenty, four-year-old White female, above average looking, slender with strawberry blonde hair, and congenial personality.

First, they interview Mrs. Wilson gathering information about Tina. She informs them she keeps employee performance records; out of the five caretakers, she ranks a number four. She has more than average tardiness, good appearance, and excellent rapport with the children. "I don't understand, I don't understand why she had her purse." "What do you mean Mrs. Wilson?"

"School policy is your purse is always kept in your locker except when using the rest room, no cell phones, it's distracting to the children.

You see we have delivery persons, lawn care, and repair services on the premises, it's for security reasons. Other than that she's a good employee, good resume and references."

In a private room, they interview Tina. Obviously, she is shaken, crying profusely, her hands are quivering. Agent Fox gives her his handkerchief. "Tina, do you want something to drink?"

"No sir." "We know this is hard for you try to calm down as much as you can, we need your assistance in finding Tony. We are going to ask you some questions, Okay." "Yeah, Okay."

Meanwhile another ransom call is made. Voice, "Get the money ready, $50,000, Okay, Tony will be returned unharmed." "Yeah, yeah, my son!" (Hang up) The call is too short to trace. The agents realize the voice is disguised.

Bee Bee being a star football player, celebrity status, the media is gathering in abundance all over the street in front of his home. A security team is called in to assist the police. Cuz reaches an agreement that they are to take orders and directions from Marvin, no problem. A yellow police security tape is put up, "POLICE DO NOT CROSS."

The interview is ongoing. Tina, tell us in as much detail as you can recall, everything that happened from the time you and the children entered the park. Her story is very much the same as reported earlier, however it's fragmented, vague and confusing. "Tina, why did you have your purse when you know it's against school policy?" "I was leaving the rest room, I knew the children were anxious to go to the park, I just wasn't thinking." "We're going to escort you to the park, Okay, you can show us what happened."

Agent Fox calls and request Jona, Blanket and Cuz to meet them at the park, before any scent Blanket may trace diminishes. Jona ask Bee Bee to give him anything of Tony's that would have a potent scent, pillow case, whatever. There has already been a long delay. Bee Bee procures a stuffed mini size doll of a football player, which Tony plays and sleeps with every night, naturally, it has a jersey #84.

Tina shows the agents the bench where she was sitting, her purse next to her. "I walked a few steps towards the kids. Suddenly, I was distracted by a couple of boys playing with one of those, you know, one of those remote-control boats. Out of the corner of my eye, I saw this male Black guy running with my purse; (pointing) that way. I chased him, shouting, "Stop him, stop him," no one responded. After a very short distance, he pitched my purse. I retrieved it, turning towards the children, they were excitedly jumping up and down screaming, "Miss Tina, Miss Tina and pointing, that man running took Tony", pointing in the opposite direction of travel. The agents think, did she call for assistance for real, or is she lying? Did she take her purse to the park on purpose? Meanwhile another ransom call comes in. Voice, "Money time, click."

Tina shows Foxy and Wright the bench she was sitting on, the direction and travel of the suspect. They return Tina to the school and transport the children to the park. At this point, the agents don't like the color of Tina's story. They realize a purse-snatcher would not discard a purse without retrieving its contents. At the park they reenact the events of what the children remember, it doesn't coincide with Tina's account of what happened.

Blanket stops at the curb exactly where the couple confirms the car was parked. Suspicions turn to a conspiracy theory at this time, in which Tina's has some involvement.

The agents begin apply the investigative approach of inductive/deductive reasoning. Did she take her purse to the park on purpose?

Back at the house the phone rings, Bee Bee answers, "Hello excitedly, his stomach churning, Wah." "Shut up, is Tony worth $50,000 to a famous football player named Bee Bee?" "Yeah uh." (Click) The agents begin to realize the people are not professionals, too many phone calls.

Bee Bee is not even told not to call to police or FBI. Professionals like a speedy conclusion. This is taking to long indicating they had a shaky plan to begin with, but are now adlibing as they go along.

The plan is for Mrs. Wilson to give Tina a week off to settle down. The agents immediately put 24/7 surveillance on her, find out who her friends and associates are and where they live. More agents are called in for assistance. Bee Bee wants to offer a $100,000 reward, Cuz wants to contribute half. The agents advise against it, informing them it would only make the ransom request larger. "They're not expecting that kind of money, they're just punks."

Finally, the phone rings again, everyone has butterflies, is antsy, scared and nervous. (Voice) "This is it, six AM tomorrow, have your dearest trusted friend go to Willow Lake with fishing gear, poles, large tackle box and a fish basket. The tackle box will contain $50,000. Set up and began fishing, got that!" "Yes sir, yes sir, got that, my son, my son!" "Yeah just shut up, I'm calling the signals for this play; observe the east side of the lake near the spillway someone will appear walking toward the wooded area. He'll light a cigarette and drop a handkerchief, go retrieve it. Wait for further instructions, got that."

(Hang up) Cuz retrieves the hander chief, which is wrapped around a cell phone. The agents receive the orders from Foxy to dismantle, abort and wait for further instructions. They are disappointed and in awe.

As Cuz enters his car, the retrieved cell phone rings, Cuz answers. (Voice) "Are you the true and trusted friend?" "I guess so." "These are your exact and immediate instructions, change of plan. Right now proceed to the Old Mill Bridge, before you arrive purchase a colorful bouquet of flowers, got that." "Yeah, then what?" "You'll find out." (Hang up) Taking a chance relaying the message on his cell phone, Cuz informs every one of his sort of standby instructions.

Foxy and his agents are taken back by these sudden changes of instructions. What should they do? Agent Fox, "We're backed into a corner, according to the map, its sixty miles from Willow Lake, time wise/other wise, we're logistically out of luck. A helicopter hovering overhead and loud above any rural area would make anyone not only curious but suspicious, no way for surveillance. Maybe we under estimated these guys."

Jona interrupts, "Sir, Mr. Foxy, Marvin's airplane!" "What?" "Marvin's small plane, no noise and could be in the area before Cuz." Agent Foxy responds, pointing his index finger at his temple in thought. "Great Jona." Marvin, "I'm out of here, be gassed up by the time you get to the airport."

Marvin, Foxy, Wright, Jona and Blanket are airborne. In route, they observe Cuz's car on the highway, time wise, its great news. The other agents are anxiously awaiting further instructions.

In flight, observing all the players from the plane, Marvin informs everyone to watch for his landing site as he descends.

Arriving at Old Mill Bridge, Cuz's new cell phone rings. (Voice) "You got money and flowers." "Yeah, yeah both, now what?" "I'll call back in five minutes, got that." Exactly five minutes later the phone rings. Cuz, "Okay what now?" "Cross the bridge on foot, approach the narrow path, walk until you see an old cemetery, turn and enter the gate, walk fifty steps straight ahead.

Place the tackle box and flowers on Willa Mae Gordon's grave marker. No tricks got that." "Okay, yeah, got that." Cuz obeys the instructions wondering, "What's happening, where is everyone?" His personal cell phone is getting nothing but static. He thinks, damn, "What am I to do?"

Circling the bridge, creek, adjacent corn field and cemetery, they observe a male individual, bib overalls, dark floppy ugly soft brimmed wavy hat emerge from the corn field, cross the creek and enter the cemetery, retrieve the tackle box check it for the money and retrace his path across the corn field, minus the flowers. As he emerges from the opposite side, he enters a green pick-up truck. It pulls off, turning in the direction of Willow Lake. Agent Fox "Were getting close, hope this is it." He begins continuous communication with the other agents. "Don't stop them until they reach a final destination. There has to be a money drop or split, there are more than two players involved in this, including Tina." "You got it chief."

Nearing Willow Lake, communications are reestablished with Cuz, he's brought up –to – date with what is happening. He's relieved of all the anguish, fear and concern he's been through, praying Tony will be safely rescued.

Unexpectedly the truck passes Willow Lake and continues west on State Route 26. Agent Fox informs all agents to prepare for an (IRO) "Immediate Response Order." Where, how much longer the agents wonder! Suddenly the pick-up turns off the highway on to a narrow trail resembling a double path with tire tracks and grass in between. "Bingo!" Agent Wright shouts. "That's the same path leading to the house they took the groceries. I'll be damn, excuse me Jona." "That's Okay, I curse too, except when I'm around Cuz an R.J." (Laughter)

Foxy calls for Back-Up realizing he is not to trust a Barney Fyfte rural area police department, after all they probably only have two or three patrol units. Agents arrive at a small cleared field where Marvin has landed. A make shift Command Post is quickly set up. The agents are informed who will approach on foot and who will approach in cars. Agents approaching on foot will surround the house. Foxy is pleased there are so many hours of daylight remaining.

Everyone is in place. As the cars approach the long double track path, Edward and Laura Gilford, are the residents of the very old somewhat dilapidated farmhouse. They sense something is wrong hearing cars approaching the house. Laura grabs Tony from a locked Room instructs her nephew Adam, a male White teenager, "Take him, quick take him, go through the corn field, hide near the creek at the old rock quarry, don't let anyone find you, go, go, right now." Chris, her other nephew, the four of them feel at this time realize their plan is falling apart. "The money, the money" she thinks, "Here Chris, here, take the money and tackle box run next door, throw it in the pond, run, run now, go, go and hide, go." Two agents emerge from a small tree lined area, tackle Chris before he reaches the pond, the money and tackle box are recovered. Chris is later identified as Tina's boyfriend from surveillance photos taken at the Burger King. He's hand cuffed to the wheel of an old ornamental chuck wagon sitting in the neighbor's yard.

Agent Fox on the radio states, "It's a Go, Go now." Agents converge on the house. Everyone is taken into custody. A search reveals, no Tony. Cuz who has by this time responded suggest to Foxy, get Jona and Blanket. They will be helpful if a search is necessary. Entering the house Blanket is somewhat passive, sniffing, not barking. Prancing down the narrow short hallway Blanket begins barking, scratching on a closed door and spinning in circles. "Something's here," Jona screams. Opening the door, they find a sort of country junk room, an old milk churn, pots, junk auto parts, etc.

On the floor is a make shift sleeping bed, ruffled blankets and a small hand pillow. Getting a scent sent from Tony's doll which Jona a brought, Blanket runs to the area, sniffing and barking then runs to a rear door, starts scratching and pawing at it. Jona opens the door, Blanket takes off running into the cornfield. Foxy, Wright, Jona, Cuz and Marvin follow behind. Reaching the creek Blanket turns sharply traveling the bank to a quarry. Climbing a steep rocky hill, he begins barking furiously into a sort of cubbyhole in the boulders. They find Adam in a squatting position cradling Tony and crying. "I like him, I wasn't going to hurt him, I wasn't."

Foxy calls Bee Bee and Thelma, Bee Bee answers the phone, "Yes, hello." "We got him, we got Tony, and he's safe, Okay!" "Yeah, oh yeah, God bless you, thank God." Everyone at the house rejoices with hugs, shouts, and hand slapping.

Chris, Tina's boyfriend is a longtime friend of Ed. A White female, Anna Butler is present, she's suspected of picking up groceries from the boarding house. Everyone is arrested and read their rights. Tina is not present.

Foxy still not trusting the local rural police calls for assistance from the State Troopers for transportation and booking at their base of operations. Returning, Tina is arrested and charged with conspiracy to kidnapping.

Tina is the first to be interrogated, she's read her rights. Agent Wright asks, "Tina, do you know how serious this situation is you've gotten yourself into?" "Am I going to jail?" "Yes, you'll be arraigned in the morning. The Judge will take it from there."

"What if I tell you everything I know, would that help?" "Maybe!" "Chris talked me into it I didn't want any part of it, he said we could make a lot of money; no one would get hurt or know I had anything to do with it." "Do you know Ed Gilford?" "No." "What about uh Laura Gilford?" "No." "Tina, tell me the whole story, the truth." Tina tells Agent Wright how she fabricated her part of what happened.

Interrogating Ed, Agent Wright states, "Ed, tell me about your involvement in the kidnapping." "Don't know nothing bout no kidnapping, got that." "Listen Ed, we've got a statement from Tina." "Don't know no Tina, got that." "What was Chris doing at your house?" "Just a friend, we use to work together, that's all." "Ed a four, year old will point to you in a "line-up" got that; a voice test of recorded phone calls will identify the caller giving instructions and requesting ransom money." "Oh, by the way Ed, did you know everyone has what are called ghost words." "Naw, what you talk'in bout?" "Words we constantly use without knowing it." "So." "So Ed, your ghost words are, "Got that," got that is going to send your ass to prison, got that! I love those words Ed, "GOT THAT."

The reunion with Tony is short lived. Cuz feels it should be a happy private family affair, everyone is elated, kisses, hugs and joyful tears, even the agents are misty eyed.

"THE ENGAGEMENT"

Time has passed, Jona and Brooke are in their sophomore year in college. Jona is pursuing a bachelor's degree in Business Administration at Norville College. Brooke a nursing degree at Hillcrest University some distance away. They periodically date, not an intimate relationship, more or less a special fondness for each other.

During Jona's junior year he becomes friends with a classmate, they study together, take pleasant walks, enjoy movies and video games. Her name is Brittney, easy to look at, well-curved, hazel eyes long wavy black hair, sort of Polynesian persuasion, intelligent, smiling personality. After sometime, the relationship develops into a loving intimate one. Serious feelings develop. Eventually Jona proposes, they become engaged. Cuz and R.J. are elated though they have never met her they are eager to welcome the occasion. They have confidence in Jona's judgment and decision-making. Brittney's parents are upper class, educated and both have above average professions. Knowing Cuz and R.J. there is an immediate invite to Brittney and her parents to visit. The happening is a pleasant one, they establish an immediate rapport, finding Brittney's parents enjoy the same social and sporting activities. Kate, Brittney's mother was a former Miss America contestant. Naturally, Brittney resembles her mother. Kate is a Public Relations manager for a large advertising firm, her father Dick is a successful realtor.

Blanket is introduced as well as Brittaney's cat Purr, they get along well. Brittney is a pet lover. Jona liking nicknames refers to Brittney as Britt. Miss "Nosey Fran" invites herself over for the occasion; naturally, she supplies her tasteful baked goodies. The outing on the lake for lunch is a new experience for Britt and her parents, dinner is fantastic. Everyone is excited about the engagement. The ladies are prematurely making wedding plans. No date has been set. Jona informs them he doesn't want a large wedding, just a private one. He doesn't want Britt exposed to a lot of so-called Fan Fare. He is out voted five to one. Britt would love the planning and excitement of a large wedding.

As time passes, apprehension grows for everyone. The date is set for June 20th; graduation is April 15th, ample time to settle down if at all possible. Jona enjoys frequent visits with Blanket, walking the coves and some loving rough housing.

The parents have decided to put off any graduation plans, the dates are to close. The focus is on the wedding. Jona has a small bachelor party, Britt a bridal shower.

Cuz has spared no expense, likewise Dick as father of the bride. It's an outdoor wedding at Cuz's home. R.J. has taken care of all the decorations, Cuz the catering, libations and entertainment. Flowers of numerous types and assorted colors adorn the grounds. Reminiscent of Cuz and R.J.'s wedding. A temporary wooden dance floor is installed, two bands, the "Lomax Band" and "Life." A well-known duo, "Just Us Two," a female vocalist Nette and her husband Gene both well-known celebrities have written two special wedding songs, they will also perform. Valet parking in a large spacious nearby lot, several dozen waiters, nothing has been overlooked. The wedding is more than extravagant, it's breath taking to more than two hundred guest.

After taking their vows, a surprise announcement is made by the newlyweds. They plan to attend veterinarian school together. After the festivities, in a private gathering with the parents, Cuz and R.J. inform them of their wedding gift. He has made arrangements for them to visit his friend's private island villa in Jamaica, the same one as before, servants and all, even a captain for the yacht. Dick and Kate present them with an extremely large monetary gift, their response is astonishment, speechless. They can even take Blanket and Purr if they wish. Both again have tears in their eyes, happy affectionate hugs and kisses.

"THE BEST GIFT EVER"

Attending veterinarian school, Jona and Britt have a moderate apartment not far from campus, Blanket and Purr live with them, and it's a happy foursome. Very little entertainment, long hours studying but they are use to studying together, it helps.

Starting their last year in veterinarian school, Cuz, having all the confidence he has in Jona, gets what he believes is a brilliant brainstorm. He purchases an attractive moderate size red brick building, bright green colorful shutters, nice grassy grounds on the edged of town not far from Lake Shore.

He keeps it a secret from everyone except R.J. He approaches his business associate Ralph and two of his investor friends, informs them of his clandestine so-called "Brilliant Plan." Reflecting on Cuz's entrepreneurial success, they are eager to come aboard. Excitement generates, enthusiasm builds immediately.

Meanwhile Brooke has married, Jona, Cuz and R.J. attended the wedding. Several months' pass, graduation nears. Jona receives a phone call, "Jona, its Brooke, guess what?" "What?" "I'm pregnant." "What, wow, uh, oh boy, Brooke, I'm so happy, and you'll be a great mother, congratulations." "Jona, it's going to be a boy." "Whatever, its great news." "Jona," a period of brief silence, you're already an uncle, (silence) now you're going to be a Godfather." "Brooke, I love you." "Same here Jona, tell everyone, Okay." "Can't wait, stay healthy." "Okay, bye."

Finally, graduation; Cuz has a pre mature plan. He calls Dick and Kate. Dick answers the phone, "Hello." "Dick, its

Cuz, is Kate there?" "Yeah, what's up?" Put her on a three-way." "Okay, she's on." "Think this over, R.J. and I would like to drive up, meet you at your house, together, drive to graduation. After the ceremony, we would like for you to come home with us, spend a couple of days together. It would be a nice time to get better acquainted, I'll have Marvin fly you home." "No further discussion necessary, sounds great, Kate's shaking her head, yes." "The kids can piggyback us back to the lake. I'll get with you on pick up and travel time, Okay." "Okay, we're on."

The graduation goes great, Jona and Britt receive their diplomas and veterinarians license. During the ride home, they stop and have a "Fast Food" lunch. Cuz has ordered a magnificent supper from his caterer to be delivered between 9:00 and 9:30 pm. Plenty of time, Cuz thinks to himself. Jona and Britt are trailing close behind. On the narrow country highway leading to the house, just on the edge of town, Cuz abruptly turns onto Erin Street. Jona wonders, "Where's he going? This is not the way to the house." Britt shrugs her shoulders in an "I don't know" gesture. Darkness has arrived. Erin Street is a moderate tree lined street mixed with small landscaped homes and small businesses.

A law office, salon and spa, insurance company, gift shop small deli and day care center. Cuz pulls his car to the curb in front of 104 Erin Street. He requests everyone to exit the cars. Bewilderment is on everyone's face.

Gathered on the sidewalk Jona ask Cuz, "What's going on?" "Just wait a second," Cuz replies making a call on his cell phone. There is a large yellow tarp covering the upper part of the building entrance. Suddenly, flood lights flash on the front of the building, two uniformed security guards exit the front door, grab two ropes, the tarp falls to the ground.

Above the door in very large gold letters are words that read: "JONA/BLANKET ANIMAL RESCUE CENTER / VETERNARIAN CLINIC."

Everyone is in awe, utter disbelief. Jona is crying loudly, falls to the ground on his knees, Britt is crying trying to comfort him. Cuz says, "Happy graduation, Jona and Britt." Everyone enters the building exploring every square foot. Jona is speechless unable to stop his joyful flowing tears. The parents leave for home. Jona and Britt inform them they'll catch up later, they want to stay and dream. Cuz tosses Jona the keys and leaves. After the first year the clinic shows phenomenal growth and profit. Blanket and Purr are daily tenants.

Cuz has turned down the movie offer realizing Jona will be to busy with the clinic. As for the book deal!

"YOU'VE JUST READ IT!"

Printed in the United States
By Bookmasters